MISTLETOE MURDER

CHRISTMAS MYSTERIES COZY MYSTERY SERIES: BOOK FOUR

MONA MARPLE

This book is dedicated to my sisters.

Thank you for being guiding lights in my life, for all of your help with A, and for believing in me and encouraging me.

I love you.

NOTICE OF DEATH

Artichoke ("Artie") Rumples passed away peacefully on Friday, 10 December 2021. He was born on 25 December, 1948.

A viewing is planned for Tuesday, 14 December 2021 at Hark Angel Church at 10am, with the funeral service to follow immediately.

Interested parties are to contact Bertram Smythe at Sleigh Bells Solicitors.

1

I looked around the streets of Candy Cane Hollow and tried to see it as an outsider would. As I had, back when I was new in the festive town.

The snow was piled high on the pavements, and the ornamental candy canes stood proud in between the ornate lampposts, as they always did.

There was a delicious fizz of excitement in the air, just as there was all over the world for Christmas. Except, in Candy Cane Hollow, every day was like Christmas.

Several of the people I passed on my journey wore Santa hats and it seemed like every shop and cafe piped out carol music.

Not to mention the fact that I was travelling in a sleigh. A real, wooden sleigh pulled by a team of reindeer.

Oh, and I was seated next to Santa. Who happened to be gorgeous and had a dimple that I often dreamed of.

My stomach flipped with nerves, and not just because of my proximity to Nick.

My sister was on her way into town to visit me and see my new home for the first time. August was my little sister, but somehow her life had always been more together than mine. She'd fallen in love, married, had a gorgeous baby boy, and kept an immaculate house.

August always looked put together because she always was put together. My approach to life had always been a bit more relaxed. I went with the flow, and often times it took me nowhere I wanted to be, but my personality just wasn't as meticulous as August's.

Despite our differences, we had always got on well. She had been my first friend and my biggest cheerleader, especially during the hard years of medical school when I had many the fantasy about escaping the studying for a tropical island or working in a bookshop.

I was excited to see her. I could barely believe she'd agreed to leave her son at home with his daddy just so we could have some quality time together.

She'd only be in town for two days, and it would be a busy 48 hours. I'd asked August to help with the final preparations for the Winter Ball, and I wasn't sure whether she was coming to see me, or to do that.

My sister sure did love organising things. She'd sent me a video of her pantry once, the contents all perfectly organised into coloured tubs, each labelled with her flawless handwriting script. It had made me side eye my own pantry (or the junk closet, as I called it) for a whole week.

"Are you sure you don't want to come with me?" I asked Nick as we approached Santa HQ.

He shook his head and gave me a smile. "I have so much to get done."

He guided the sleigh to a stop, leaned across and planted a gentle, warm kiss on my forehead. I closed my eyes and murmured my enjoyment. Every time Nick kissed me I wanted to pinch myself that he was really mine. My boyfriend! My stomach fluttered just at the thought.

"Well you have a great time, okay? I can't wait to meet your sister tonight," he said as he climbed out of the sleigh and walked to the front, where he looked sternly at Einstein, the trainee reindeer. He addressed the animal in his toughest voice, "No hijinks now, alright?"

I could have sworn the young animal gave an embarrassed nod. This year would be the first time Einstein was in the Christmas Eve reindeer team, and the excitement had got the better of him on occasion. Nothing too serious had happened, as long as you didn't count him careering into the snow pit while Old Bum McGhee was practicing a new snowman building technique. He'd almost finished a 12ft high masterpiece when Einstein trotted in and sent the snow tumbling everywhere.

I waved goodbye to Nick and then lingered on the pretence that I was getting the reins straight in my hands. Really, I just wanted to watch him. I could watch that man all day long. No sooner had he began to climb the steps to the building than the main door flew open and his elf assistant, Mitzy, greeted him with her Clipboard of Jobs and Demands, as Nick called it.

I laughed to myself and then commanded the reindeer to move on. Away we sped towards the Tinsel Transport depot, where I was assured my sister would be waiting. How exactly she would get to Candy Cane Hollow, I didn't know. The place was just 40 minutes outside of London, and yet it appeared to be protected by magic that meant it could only be discovered if someone here wanted it to be.

Whatever the requirements were, August had passed them all, and was about to discover not only that Santa was real, but that I was dating him.

It was a lot to take in, especially for someone with a practical mind, like my sister.

As I approached the depot, I saw August shivering against the cold. I'd told her to wrap up but she must not have believed that there would be snow here when London was enjoying a typically wet, but mild, day. A huge, bulky suitcase stood on either side of her, and I said a silent thank you that I'd brought one of the bigger sleighs out.

August spotted me and burst out laughing, then waved both hands in the air as if I might not notice her standing there, all alone.

"Oh my gosh! Look at you! Look at this? Is this a... sleigh?" August asked in between her laughter. She looked at the reindeer and reached out to stroke Betty. I groaned.

"I don't think so, ma'am. We've not even been introduced," Betty said.

August shot backwards and scanned the depot building for hidden cameras. "Is this a prank?"

"No," I said. I offered a weak smile and saw the confusion on my sister's face. "Shall we get a drink?"

August gave the reindeers a wary look but nodded at me. I wasn't ready to introduce August to the hustle and bustle of the High Street, but thankfully the depot had a small and rarely used cafe.

The automatic doors opened and an elderly elf dashed across the snow as quick as he could. Norbert, I read from his tag. "Sorry for the wait, Dr Wood, there's a rush on inside. Shall I park this up for you?"

"Yes, please. That would be really helpful," I said as I climbed down from the sleigh and handed the reins over to Norbert. He had grabbed a suitcase in each hand and tossed those back in the hold with impressive and surprising strength.

I learned more and more often to never underestimate an elf.

While he went off to park the sleigh, I tucked an arm through August's and lead her into the building, where I saw that the cafe rush meant that two of the five tables were occupied.

Since Norbert was the valet and the barista, we showed ourselves to a table. We'd order drinks when he returned.

"I'm so glad you're here," I enthused.

"I'm so glad you invited me. This place is something else, Hol. How did you even find it?" August asked.

I picked at one of my fingernails. A bad habit I'd had from childhood. "I crashed my car in a snowbank and..."

"You what? Are you okay?" The concern was written all over my sister's face and I felt a flood of love for her wash over me. It was so good to have her here.

"I'm fine. Mrs Claus rescued me and brought me here."

"Mrs Claus brought you to this magical wonderland. You realise how crazy that all sounds?" August asked, her eyes wide with concern.

I took a deep breath. "Yes. I realise it sounds very crazy, but it's true. This place really is magical. It's the home of Christmas."

"I can see that!" August laughed. Even the small transport depot was decorated to the nines, with an enormous Christmas tree taking up the majority of the available space right in the middle of the open waiting area.

"Mrs Claus, the lady who rescued me, she really is Mrs Claus. She's married to Father Christmas."

"Okay," August drew the word out, as if she didn't believe a word I was saying but wasn't going to argue with me. Maybe she thought I still had concussion from the car crash.

"Father Christmas has retired from active Santa work. He's been training his son."

August shrugged. "I guess we all have to retire eventually."

I nodded. "It's a big responsibility and the hours are really long. Especially on Christmas Eve, that's an all-nighter."

August gave me a smile that I couldn't read. I needed to just get it all said, out in the open, and then I'd take her to see for herself that I was telling the truth.

"So Nick is the new Santa," the words tumbled out quickly.

August narrowed her eyes. "Nick? Hold on, you mean Mr Hunka-licious?"

I nodded reluctantly. Nick had no idea that my sister had given him such a pet name.

"You're dating Santa?" August asked.

Again, I nodded. What could I say?

After a few seconds of silence, August clapped her hands over her mouth. "This is so wild!"

"Wait. You believe me?" I asked.

August laughed. "Of course I do. You haven't lied to me since you were a child and you pretended you didn't have a crush on Billy Branson."

"And you're okay with it?"

"Well, I'm going to need to meet Mr Hunkalicious and give him my approval but... wait. Do I have a crush on Santa? Is that... allowed?"

I giggled. "Well, I definitely have a crush on Santa."

I cleared my throat as I realised that Norbert was hanging around near the table, a festive notepad and a novelty snowman pen poised ready to take down our orders.

"We're going to head into town now, actually. But thank you," I said apologetically.

Norbert gave a slow nod of his head. "I'll go and fetch your sleigh, Dr Wood. I really am rushed off my feet today!"

We watched the old elf totter off and waited outside for him to pull up with the sleigh. I thanked him and he disappeared back to the heady rush of two customers at the same time.

"Now, let me do the introductions. Betty, Einstein, Donna, Matix, please meet my sister August," I said. The reindeer looked at my sister with varying levels of interest. Einstein was repeating her name under his breath to help him memorise it, while Donna deliberately looked away and refused to engage. Being named in the famous song had done nothing to keep her ego in check. Matix gave her his best attempt at an alluring smile and winked at her, and Betty leaned in close and gave my sister a good sniff.

"Chanel?" Betty asked. She had a fierce love of perfume and was never wrong in naming one.

August flushed and nodded. "My husband buys me a bottle for our anniversary every year."

Betty swooned at the notion of such romance, while Matix rolled his eyes at the realisation that August wasn't single.

"I'm sorry I tried to stroke you without asking. That was very rude of me. I've just never stroked a reindeer before," August explained. I heard that she was using her telephone voice, as we called it. The voice all British people reserved for when we wanted to make a good first impression.

"You can stroke me now, if I can share some of that perfume with you later," Betty proposed.

August giggled and the deal was done. Betty leaned in and

allowed August to run her fingers through her coat. It was shaggy and coarse no matter how many times Betty convinced us to try the latest and greatest shampoo on it.

August reached into her handbag and pulled out the tiny bottle of Chanel No5. Betty gasped, snorted and whinnied in excitement, then stood perfectly still while August sprayed some on her. Einstein began to sneeze. He was allergic to everything.

"I will guard you with my life," Betty said, and ducked her head as if she was greeting royalty.

I laughed. "Come on, let's get into town. My sister needs the grand tour and I know nobody does it better than you guys."

We climbed up into the sleigh and August oohed and aahed at the craftsmanship that had gone in to building the hand carved structure. I draped a fleece blanket over her lap and tucked it in. Once we started to trot up a speed, she'd feel the chill.

2

Following the tour of Candy Cane Hollow, we returned to Claus Cottage. My apartment didn't have enough space for me to host a guest, so August and I would be sharing a bedroom at Claus Cottage.

I was giddy with excitement about this. August and I had shared a bedroom growing up and I had fond memories of the nights we would lie whispering to each other after lights out.

"So, I'm going to meet the in laws?" August asked.

My cheeks flamed. "Not quite. Mrs Claus is desperate for Nick to get married, but it's not something we've discussed. We're taking it slow."

August raised an eyebrow. "You're dating Santa and you want to take it slow? You need to get a ring on it, sis!"

I gave a nervous laugh, suddenly terrified at the prospect of August and Mrs Claus tag teaming.

I shuddered as my imagination transformed them into some kind of two-headed Bridezilla.

"I'm just enjoying each day as it comes," I said.

August pulled a face. "I like to enjoy each day as I plan it out in my Erin Condren."

I had no idea what that meant, so I pushed open the heavy front door of Claus Cottage.

"Helloooooo?" I called out to signal our arrival. I knew that Mrs Claus was planning on asking Gilbert to prepare some kind of welcome dinner, and didn't want to catch the elf by surprise.

"Oh, Holly!" Exclaimed Ginger Rumples as she emerged from the living room and dove into my arms. I gave a nervous laugh as I hugged Nick's oldest friend.

"Are you okay?" I asked. Ginger and I got on fine, but she wasn't usually so physically affectionate. As she pulled away from me I saw that her red mane of hair was tangled and her eyes were watery.

"There's been a death in the family," she said, then noticed my sister standing beside me. "Oh, I'm sorry. You must be Holly's sister?"

"I'm August. I'm so sorry for your loss," my sister said, because of course she knew the perfect words of sympathy to offer. She probably had a condolence card tucked into her luggage just in case the occasion arose.

"It's okay. I mean, as okay as someone dying ever is. Artie was old. I just came over to ask Mrs Claus if some of the relatives could stay here when they arrive for the funeral."

"I'm sure there's space."

"That's what she said. Look, I have to get going, but let's have a proper catch up soon?"

"Sounds good," I agreed.

"Take care of yourself," August said with a concerned smile.

Ginger thanked her and disappeared out of the front door and back into the snowy afternoon.

"That's really sad. She seems nice, though," August said.

I nodded. "She and Nick have been best friends since they were both tiny."

August giggled. "I still can't believe you're dating Santa! You have such a glamorous life!"

I raised a doubtful eyebrow. August had always been the one with the glamorous life, in fact her life looked perfect from the outside.

But I was old enough and wise enough to know that nothing was truly perfect.

"It was good of Tom to let you come," I said, then winced as I heard how my words sounded. August didn't need his permission, of course, but she did need him to be on single parent duty while she was away.

She shrugged. "He's been working such long hours. I think he's looking forward to some quality time with Jeb. When I'm there, he just wants his mama, you know?"

"Of course. Why wouldn't he?" I said with a smile.

A crash came from the kitchen and I scurried down the hallway, with August right behind me. In the kitchen there was quite the scene. Gilbert stood by the fridge, staring down at a pile of cake tins that were scattered over the floor.

"Do you need any help?" I asked.

"Help? Oh! I'm an elf who needs help now, am I? Poor old Gilbert, useless and washed up! Why don't I just hang up my apron strings and be done?! Oh. You're new," Gilbert said as he spotted August partway through his rant.

"I'm August, Holly's sister," she introduced.

"A doctor too, are you?" Gilbert asked.

August laughed. "Nothing that grand. I'm a housewife. And a mum! I have a baby back home."

"A housewife, you say?" Gilbert asked, his interest peaked.

August gave a nod.

"Hmm. And what's your stance on apple cider vinegar?" Gilbert asked, his lips pursed and arms crossed as he grilled my sister.

"I love it. I use it for everything. It gets out stains and cleans surfaces, and I even drink a tablespoon of it each morning," August said.

Gilbert visibly relaxed as if she had passed some kind of test. He eyed August carefully then burst into a grin. "You and I are going to get along like baubles on a tree!"

"Oh!" August said as her cheeks flushed. "I'm glad to hear it! Do you need a hand with anything?"

As quick as anything, Gilbert's eyes narrowed again. "Do I need a hand? What about me makes you think I need help? Or has Holly told you something? Is that it? She's warned you that I keep a dirty kitchen, has she? I've got a mind to find Mrs Claus and hand in my..."

"Gilbert. Do give our visitor a moment to get her bearings," Mrs Claus scolded from behind us.

August and I both turned and saw that Mrs Claus was dressed in her full ceremonial Claus outfit, consisting of a heavy red twinset lined with white fur. She looked every inch the wife of Father Christmas, and I saw August take her in with a gaping mouth.

"Hello, August, dear. You'll want to close your mouth before you catch flies," Mrs Claus said with a wink.

"Flies! I'll have you know there are no flies in my kitchen!" Gilbert exclaimed from the kitchen as he picked up the cake tins and placed them in the sink to wash.

"Of course, dear. It's just an expression," Mrs Claus called to him.

"Expressions like that lead to reputations being ruined," Gilbert muttered under his breath.

"Now, August, you've had the tour and you've met our beloved Gilbert. You may want to relax for a while. We have some additional guests arriving this evening."

"We saw Ginger. She told us a relative has passed away," I said.

Mrs Claus nodded. "Had you heard of Artie?"

I shook my head.

"That's not surprising. He was an eccentric. He kept himself to himself. He lived alone in a shack over on Mistletoe Moor."

"And he was related to Ginger?" I asked. I'd never heard her speak of him before.

Mrs Claus cocked her head to one side and stuck her tongue out, as if trying to calculate something. "A second uncle twice removed or something like that. The Rumples family makes up a good portion of Candy Cane Hollow. It's impossible to keep track of all of the relationships."

"But Ginger wants his family to stay here?"

"Artie was a very wealthy man. Very well respected by the community. He was the owner of Festive Feast."

I stared at her blankly.

"The company that makes all of the frozen Christmas dinner ready meals. They're very popular with the hospital, nursing homes, all of those people who want a Christmas dinner but can't cook one."

"I haven't heard of them," I said.

"That's because you have an elf who works himself into the ground to prepare your meals!" Gilbert called out from the kitchen.

Mrs Claus rolled her eyes. "Let's go into the den."

We followed her into the cosy space, filled with comfortable chairs and warmed by an open fire.

"So Artie's family want to be hosted by the Claus family because of Artie's wealth?" August asked as she lowered herself daintily into an armchair.

"I'd imagine so. And we have the space, so we're happy to oblige."

"Are you sure there's still room for us? Because we can stay in my flat if it's easier," I offered.

Mrs Claus shook her head. "Nonsense. Of course there's room. We have more room than we can possibly use in this place. I believe it's only Artie's son and daughter in law coming, anyway."

There was a rap at the front door and Mrs Claus jumped up from her seat. "Ah, I bet that'll be them now."

She padded across the den towards the door, but Gilbert had got there first.

"You can't just turn up here! Do you have an appointment to see Mrs Claus?" he asked.

"Gilbert! Gosh, nobody needs an appointment to see me. Let them in, dear!" Mrs Claus said.

I peeked through the open den door and saw a small female elf walk in, her gaze downcast. She trembled with the cold, which wasn't a surprise. She wore a pair of green leggings and a red tabard, and although the look was very festive, it wasn't weather appropriate.

"Patrice, what a wonderful surprise," Mrs Claus exclaimed.

"You should ring first in future," Gilbert moaned, then stood up straight and made his way back towards the kitchen. "I'll make drinks!"

Mrs Claus ushered the elf into the den and gestured for her to take a seat. The elf glanced at me and August and gave us a shy smile.

"Is this a social visit, dear?"

"Oh! No, no. I'd never stop by just to say hello, Mrs Claus. I know how busy you are with the Winter Ball preparations."

"Actually, Holly here is handling that," Mrs Claus said, and beamed at me from across the room.

I could feel August grow jittery with excitement just from the mention of the event she would be helping organise the finishing touches for.

"Oh. Well, still. There is a reason I'm here. I need advice, Mrs Claus, and there's nobody I respect more..."

"That's awfully kind of you to say, dear. I'd be honoured to help if I can. What is it?"

Any reply Patrice planned on giving didn't come, because there was another rap on the door. Patrice jumped at the sound and cowered in the chair.

"I'll get it... again!" Gilbert called. He opened the door, then closed it again. The knocking persisted.

"Gilbert? What's got into you?" Mrs Claus asked as she got to her feet.

"This can't go on! There's no room at the inn. We can't have every waif and stray showing up here without notice!"

"We'll discuss this later," Mrs Claus said in the sternest voice I'd ever heard her use.

She opened the front door herself and exclaimed as an angry elf barged into Claus Cottage and dripped snow all across the floor as he came right into the den and stared straight at Patrice.

"Home. Now."

"Rudy, please," Patrice begged.

"What is the meaning of this?" Mrs Claus asked, but Rudy paid her no attention. Gilbert appeared in the den doorway, a scowl on his face.

"I won't forgive you for bringing drama to my door, Patrice!" He said.

"Let's go," Rudy said again.

Patrice shook her head and sank further into the seat.

"Now, listen dears. It's clear that emotions are running high. I think the best thing is that you both stay here. We have enough guest rooms."

"She's my wife, and if I say she's coming home, that's what she's doing," Rudy said.

"I can promise you she's going nowhere if she doesn't want to. Now enough of the bully boy tactics. Gilbert, please take Rudy upstairs and have a room made up for him. I'm sure he'll feel calmer after a nice shower and a bowl of your chicken soup."

Gilbert was less than impressed with the idea but didn't argue. With a scowl directed at Rudy, he turned and left the room, and Rudy followed.

As soon as they were gone, Patrice began to cry. "I'm so sorry. Gilbert's right, I shouldn't be here. I had no idea Rudy was coming after me."

"His behaviour is out of control," August murmured.

Patrice nodded. "That's why we separated. It was only a few weeks ago and he hasn't got the message yet that it's permanent."

"Is that what you need our help with, dear?" Mrs Claus asked.

Patrice shook her head. "No, no... I've got something of a..."

She was interrupted again by a knock at the door, and since Gilbert was upstairs getting Rudy settled, Mrs Claus rose and answered the door.

"Sprout! Brandy! How lovely to see you. I'm just sorry it's under these dreadful circumstances," Mrs Claus greeted.

She returned to the den with a couple behind her. The man had a ruddy complexion and was dressed in a fur coat. The woman had severe eyebrows and white hair secured in a high bun.

"Come on in and take a seat. I'll make drinks while you relax for a while. Was the journey okay, Sprout, dear?"

The man shrugged. "The boat was late but that's happening more and more often."

"There's a shortage of river elves. I don't know how your father stayed out there for so long, in the middle of nowhere," the woman said with a sneer.

"There really is a wonderful community spirit on Mistletoe Moor, Brandy. I'm sure Artie was well looked after out there," Mrs Claus reassured them, then left the room to make drinks. There was no need to take our order. Hot chocolate was the drink for every occasion in Candy Cane Hollow.

"What time is it?" Sprout asked his wife.

She glanced at a thick gold watch. "We have an hour before the meeting. One of you can probably take us into town?"

August and I looked at each other as we realised that Brandy was talking to us. Did she think we were staff?

"I'm sure a ride can be organised. I don't believe we've met. I'm Holly and this is my sister August. And over there..." I gestured towards Patrice's chair, but the elf had disappeared. How strange.

"This is a difficult time for us and we really don't have the capacity for small talk," Sprout said as he offered us a tight lipped smile.

"Of course," August and I said in unison.

"So, where's Nick?" August whispered.

"He's at work. He'll be home in time for dinner. What do you think to everything so far?"

She beamed at me. "It's incredible. I hope I can bring Jeb here one day. He'd love to see this place."

"I'm sure that can be arranged," I said as my heart soared. My sister was with me in Candy Cane Hollow, and she was taking all of its magic and revelations in her stride!

Mrs Claus returned to the room with a tray of hot chocolates, and set them out on the coffee table for us all.

August and I said thank you. The newly bereaved guests sitting across from us didn't. My heart ached for them. They must be overwhelmed with grief.

"Mrs C, we have to get into town shortly," Sprout said.

"We have an important meeting," Brandy added.

"Of course, dear. We'll make sure a sleigh is ready and waiting. Do you need any help with the arrangements for tomorrow?"

Tomorrow? The Winter Ball was the day after, but I hadn't heard of anything happening tomorrow.

"The funeral's all planned. Father left his wishes with the funeral director. It was all prepaid, too," Sprout said.

"Artie was such a practical man," Mrs Claus said with a smile.

"You knew him well?" Brandy seemed surprised by the idea.

"We volunteered together for the Chamber of Cheer & Commerce. That's going back quite some time, though."

Sprout snorted. "It would have to be. He's barely left his shack in the last twenty years."

"Well, we all need some alone time, I guess," Mrs Claus said and offered her brightest smile.

Gilbert appeared in the doorway then, took one look at the drinks that had been prepared by someone other than himself, huffed, and left again.

August allowed a quiet giggle out. "I want to take that elf home with me."

"Don't say that too often, dear. I might agree," Mrs Claus said with a wink, then turned her attention back to Sprout and Brandy. "Now, where is it you need to get to?"

"Sleigh Bells Solicitors. They're on the High Street," Sprout explained.

Mrs Claus nodded. "Will you be okay in a sleigh? I could always drive you over myself."

"Yes, please. If you don't mind," Sprout said.

"Of course not. I'll just go and powder my nose."

The four of us sat in an awkward silence until Mrs Claus returned to the room, at which point Sprout and Brandy rose from the loveseat. Neither had touched their hot chocolates. It was just as well Gilbert hadn't made them or his confidence would be shattered.

"Ready when you are," Mrs Claus said.

It was far too early to set off for an appointment in an hour's time, but Sprout and Brandy hastily made it clear that they were ready, and the three of them set off.

As soon as they'd left, Patrice returned to the room. She looked at the abandoned hot chocolates, downed one and then downed the second. A chocolate moustache decorated her upper lip.

"Oh, they weren't yours, were they?" She asked. She had the demeanour and the squeaky voice of a mouse and I tried to sit very still so I didn't startle her.

"No, they were just sitting there going to waste," I said with a smile.

"Wh-where's Mrs Claus?"

"She took Sprout and Brandy into town," I said. "It sounded earlier like you needed to talk. Is there anything we can do to help you? Mrs Claus might be some time."

"Oh, no. I'll wait for her," Patrice said.

Gilbert returned to the room and eyed us each in turn, his gaze deciding to focus on Patrice. "You'd better not have brought any drama here."

"Gilbert!" I exclaimed. The elf could always be dramatic, but it wasn't like him to be so outwardly rude.

"It's okay," Patrice said.

"No it isn't. You're a guest here at Claus Cottage and you'll be treated with respect," I said.

Gilbert's face blanched. "Forgive me. Holly is right. Mrs Claus invited you in and I respect nothing more in this world than Mrs Claus."

"It's really okay. I know I've got you wrapped up in some bad decisions over the years, but I swear that's all behind me," Patrice said.

I looked from one of them to the other. There was something of a resemblance between them. "You two know each other?"

"Patrice is my cousin. Or one of eight dozen, anyway. She's got me involved in some real scrapes over the years."

"I've told you I'm sorry about that night," Patrice whispered.

"It's not the kind of thing I can forget easily!" Gilbert exclaimed.

"It was 2am!"

"And what does that matter?" Gilbert asked.

"What happened?" August asked. She was leaning forward in her chair, looking like a person desperate to know about a plot twist.

Gilbert avoided her gaze. "It only happened once."

"And it was my fault," Patrice volunteered.

"Go on," August encouraged.

"I... I can't bring myself to say it. If Mrs Claus hears about it..."

"Gilbert left the dirty dishes overnight!" Patrice said the words so quick they came out sounding like one long word.

Gilbert's head hung in shame, but his pointed ears were bright red and betrayed his embarrassment.

"That's it?" I asked with a laugh.

"I realised at 4am I was never going to get to sleep, so I got back up and did them," Gilbert said.

"He did. He was cleaning those plates with so much rage he woke the rest of us up," Patrice said with a firm nod of her head.

"Those were in my heady student days. Everything gets a little out of control. I can assure you I've learned the error of my ways since then," Gilbert said.

"I'm sure you have," I said as I tried to stifle a laugh. It was clearly a touchy subject for Gilbert, and one he blamed Patrice for. "Why do you blame Patrice for it?"

"I blame myself! But Patrice and I always got on so well. She had this way of making me forget about my responsibilities that nobody else could. We stayed up too late chatting, and that's not a way I could carry on living."

"That's why we don't see each other any more," Patrice murmured.

"Wait. You stopped seeing your cousin because you have fun together? That's exactly what relatives are supposed to do," August said. "Trust me, Holly and I have some crazy times behind us, and hopefully more ahead of us."

"But August, talk to me housekeeper to housekeeper. You don't worry that all of that fun and frivolity will lead to disaster?" Gilbert asked, his eyes wide.

"Disaster like leaving dirty dishes for a couple of hours?"

"It could be any kind of disaster! You could go to the shop without a list, or forget to thaw the turkey for dinner. There are endless opportunities for the whole thing to go to ruin," Gilbert exclaimed.

"I guess I'm not in the same league of housekeeping as you," August said with a shrug.

Gilbert narrowed his eyes. "But I feel a deep connection to you. Tell me, do you add Zoflora to your steam mop?"

August laughed. "Yes."

"Even though the directions warn against it?"

August shrugged and pulled a face. "I guess I didn't read the directions."

Gilbert gasped and appeared to make the sign of the cross on his body. "Santa help us. It seems you're right, we're not two of a kind at all."

3

Mrs Claus returned with Sprout and Brandy, and the guests retired to their room without a single word to August and me.

We were still in the den with Patrice, and Rudy had joined us. We sat in an awkward silence. It was clear that Rudy wanted to speak to Patrice privately, and it was clear that she didn't want that. For that reason, August and I stayed where we were.

"Ah, it's so lovely to have a house full of guests to entertain. Just wait until dinner! Gilbert will have prepared a feast, no doubt," Mrs Claus said as she popped her head into the den.

"I really need to talk to you before dinner," Rudy told Patrice.

She gestured to the room with her hands open and wide. "You can speak now."

"It's of a personal nature," he said.

Snowy, Mrs Claus' white cat, jumped up onto August's lap and she began to stroke the creature rhythmically.

"Does the cat talk as well?"

I shook my head. "You shouldn't have even heard the reindeer talk. I've only been able to in the last few weeks."

"What do you mean?"

"Only true believers can hear them. It's all part of the Christmas magic. To be honest, I thought you'd have grown out of believing."

"Me? Never! Or, maybe I did, but having a child makes it pretty impossible not to believe in the magic of Christmas. I have to bring Jeb here."

I grinned. It made me so happy that my sister was enjoying my new home, and planning a return visit.

"I would love that," I said, and I squeezed her hand.

The front door opened then, and in walked none other than Mr Hunkalicious himself. He lit up with a grin as soon as he saw me, and he and that darn dimple winked away at me.

"August, this is Nick," I said as soon as I got my heart rate under control.

Nick was dressed in a casual pair of jeans and flannel shirt, and judging by the way my sister's cheeks reddened, she approved of him as much as I'd hoped she would.

"Finally, I get to meet the famous August!" Nick exclaimed, and he strode across the room and pulled her into a hug.

"You smell like Christmas," she whimpered as they parted.

He laughed. "Hazard of the job, I'm afraid."

I saw his gaze skip across to Patrice and Rudy, and jumped in to rescue him. He didn't share Mrs Claus' talent for remembering everyone in town by name.

"Nick, this is Patrice and Rudy. I'm sure you remember that Patrice is one of Gilbert's cousins," I introduced.

Nick flashed me a grateful smile, then greeted the elves with his booming voice and a strong handshake.

"He's incredible. That dimple. Lord have mercy," August whispered.

I laughed.

"Does Gilbert know you're here?" Nick asked.

Patrice shook her head. "I'm not here to see him. I need some advice from your mum, but I know she's busy entertaining right now."

"Oh, she's never too busy to help someone in need. Especially one of Gilbert's relatives. His family is our family, after all," Nick said with a warm smile.

"I'll go and look for her," I offered.

"I'll come," August said.

We left the den and peeked into the kitchen, where it appeared that Gilbert was preparing a full Christmas dinner with all the trimmings. The smell was amazing and I suddenly felt very hungry.

Mrs Claus wasn't in there, though, and so we walked upstairs towards Mrs Claus' office. She was seated at her desk, concentrating on writing something.

I coughed to alert her to our presence.

"Oh! Holly dear, I'm sorry. The time has got away from me. Come in, come in. You too, August, dear. I promise I don't usually shut myself away like this," she said with a grin.

I glanced at the notepad which contained multiple crossings out. "What are you working on?"

"Sprout has asked me to deliver a speech at Artie's funeral tomorrow," she explained.

"It looks like you're struggling," I said.

She nodded. "The family aren't going to say anything, so I'm feeling the pressure to get everything across."

"Why isn't Sprout making a speech?" I asked.

"Oh, grief affects everyone differently. Sprout didn't exactly see eye to eye with his father. They'd been estranged for many years. Maybe he feels it's not his place, under the circumstances."

"Oh, that's a shame," August murmured.

"It's a trying time. I get the impression the meeting at the solicitors went badly, as well."

"It did?" I asked.

Mrs Claus shrugged. "There was an atmosphere in the sleigh on the way back. Neither of them said a word all the way here. And they just disappeared off to their room right away. I do hope they haven't had more bad news."

A loud bell rang out from downstairs, signalling that dinner was ready.

Mrs Claus grinned at us. "Perfect timing. I'm so hungry I could eat a skinny reindeer. This speech can wait until later."

It took a few minutes to round everyone up, but eventually we were all seated at the grand dining table and Gilbert did the honours of serving us portions of everything. He piled moist roasted turkey on my plate, then mashed potatoes, honeyed carrots, Brussels sprouts, peas, cabbage and a Yorkshire pudding, followed by lashings of gravy.

The smell was heavenly and I groaned, then laughed when August did exactly the same thing.

"I can't remember the last time anyone cooked for me. Thank you, Gilbert," she said.

Gilbert stood perfectly still and looked at her, as if waiting for a punchline or a note of sarcasm. When he realised she was being serious, he began to sniffle into the gravy.

Nick sat across from me and caught my eye, and I felt my cheeks flame.

"Shall we take a moment before we start eating and just think about poor Artie, who is no longer with us. He lived a life of service and will be greatly missed."

Sprout had already lifted a spoonful of mashed potato to his mouth and attempted to swallow it discreetly.

"Maybe you could tell us some stories about your dad? If that wouldn't be too painful?" I asked.

Sprout looked at me with an expression that was unreadable. "There really isn't too much to say about the old man. He started a business and that's really the reason anyone here cared about him. He created jobs and all that good stuff. But in reality, he was odd. I happen to believe that he lost his mind in the last few years."

Mrs Claus gasped. "You do? Oh, that's awful."

"It is."

"You're sure of it?"

"Someone had taken advantage of him. I should have expected it, really. A man of his wealth. He was no stranger to a begging letter but normally knew to ignore them."

"Sprout, maybe this isn't the time," Brandy murmured at his side.

"Yeah, nobody wants to hear about an old dead guy's drama," Rudy said from across the table. Patrice sat next to him, perfectly still, her senses heightened as if she may need to make a quick escape.

"I'm sorry, but who the heck are you two anyway?" Sprout asked as he looked across at the elves.

"I'm Rudy. I'm the guy to come to for any last minute event tickets. You need some for the Winter Ball, I'm your elf," he said with pride.

"Unless you want real tickets, as opposed to fakes. Rudy specialises in counterfeit tickets," Gilbert said. He had been convinced to sit and eat with us for once, but I noticed that his own food was untouched and suspected he would eat alone in the kitchen after everyone else was done.

"That was a one off! My supplier sold me duds. I knew nothing about it!" Rudy protested.

"And who's she?" Sprout pointed towards Patrice with his fork.

"Ah, now this is my better half..."

"I'm not your wife," Patrice whispered.

"Legally, you are," Rudy said.

"Only because you won't sign the papers," Patrice said.

Rudy sighed. "We're in a slight state of flux right now. But this is my wife, Patrice."

"Patrice?" Sprout dropped his cutlery on the table with a clatter and stared at the elf, who looked down at the table.

"That's a fairly unusual name, right?" Brandy asked.

"She's the only Patrice in Candy Cane Hollow. Her mother sees it as something of a personal mission to keep the family names unique," Gilbert explained.

"Is that right?" Sprout asked.

Gilbert nodded. "You should see their side of the family tree. They have a Gingerbread, a Unicorn, a Candyfloss and even..."

"I think you and I should have a little chat, huh, Patrice?" Sprout interrupted.

Patrice shook her head. "I don't think so."

"Oh, I insist. I'd love to know how you knew my father."

"I didn't," Patrice said. She finally lifted her gaze and looked across the table, but her hands were shaking.

"Patrice, dear, are you okay?" Mrs Claus asked.

Patrice began to cry. "I need your help, Mrs Claus."

"You can get all the help you need later. But right now I need to know how you knew my father?" Sprout repeated.

Patrice took a deep breath and met his gaze. "I just told you. I didn't. I never met him in my life, I swear."

"Then would you care to explain to me why my father's Will leaves every single thing he owned to you?"

4

Nick managed to convince Sprout to go for a walk and cool down, and Brandy followed hot on his heels.

With those two out of the way, we all returned to the den and Patrice gave up any attempt to stop the tears coming. She really did make a sorry figure, hunched over her tiny frame. She was a trembling mess.

"Is this what you came to tell us, dear?" Mrs Claus asked.

Patrice snivelled and gave a quick nod of her head.

"So what Sprout said is true? You're the beneficiary of Artie's Will?" Mrs Claus asked.

"He always was a crafty one! What a fun little puzzle he's left us with," Rudy gave a laugh and began to rub his hands together.

"It doesn't feel very fun to me. I-I-I don't know why he's picked me!"

"How did you find out about it?" August asked.

"There was a letter posted to me. No, not posted..."

"It couldn't have been posted. The Polar Delivery Service is awfully slow at this time of year," Nick said.

"Their budgets keep being cut, year after year. I've told your father to have a look into it," Mrs Claus said, then returned her attention to Patrice. "So, the letter wasn't posted?"

"It must have been hand delivered. I woke up and it was there on the doormat. I assumed it must be a menu for the new takeaway turkey place, it seems like I get three of those a week."

"Hmm. Us too, dear," Mrs Claus clucked sympathetically.

"Well, the details don't matter really, do they? Good old Artie made his Will and we're quids in!" Rudy said with a grin.

"This is nothing to do with you, Rudy. I don't even know why you're here. We're not a couple any longer," Patrice picked at her fingernails as she spoke.

"You wanted a bit of time apart and we've had that. Plus, you have to admit, our problems can all be sorted with this kind of money!"

"How much are we talking?" I asked, then covered my mouth with my hand. What kind of a crass question had I just asked?!

"I d-d-don't know," Patrice said. "The letter just said the whole estate was left to me. It's a lot, right?! There was the business, and rumour has it that Artie never spent any money. He lived out in that shack."

"Even better!" Rudy exclaimed. His eyes were bulging and huge, no doubt as he pictured all of the things he could spend the money on.

"It will be a considerable amount, yes. You've just become a very wealthy woman, Patrice. Now, how exactly did you think I could help with that?" Mrs Claus asked, her expression kind.

Patrice shrugged. "I-I-I wanted to know if he had family, but now I know he did. Why didn't he leave everything to his son?"

Mrs Claus adopted a sad smile. "He was estranged from Sprout for many years. There was some argument. Sprout has quite the explosive temper and he just cut Artie off completely."

"That's really sad," Patrice said. "I can't stand to think of that poor old man living out in that shack all alone."

The door opened and Gilbert walked in with a round of fresh hot chocolates for everyone.

He eyed his cousin warily, seemingly uncomfortable with his work and his personal life mixing in such a way.

"Mrs Claus, I have to promise you that I had no idea she was going to just show up here," he said as he served her first.

She batted his concerns away with a chuckle. "Gilbert, dear, family comes first. Just because you're very much a part of this family doesn't mean you aren't still part of your biological family. Poor Patrice has had quite the shock."

"I'd imagine she has. Discovering that a local billionaire has left all of his earthly goods to her! Imagine how many bottles of bleach I could buy with that…"

"B-b-billionaire?"

"Billionaire? With a b? Blimey! Now we're talking!" Rudy said as he snatched a hot chocolate from the decorative tray and downed it in one.

"I don't think Artie was quite that wealthy, Gilbert," Mrs Claus said.

Gilbert shrugged. "That's what Yule Believe It is saying."

I rolled my eyes. "We've told you about that gossip column before. It's never based on real information."

Gilbert hovered in the doorway, clearly waiting for something.

"Thank you, Gilbert. Excellent hot chocolates and impeccable service, as always, dear," Mrs Claus complimented.

Pleased with the words, Gilbert stood straighter, puffed out his chest and left the room.

"I'd invite him to join us but he'd only see it as some suggestion that he's work shy," Mrs Claus said with a wink.

"Oh, it's so much to take in!" Patrice wailed.

"Are you wondering whether to keep the money or not?" I asked.

"Hold on, now! There's no need for that! What kind of question is that? The old man made his wishes clear. Who are we to get meddling?!" Rudy jumped to his seat, his face red. There was something intimidating about him and I shrank back in my chair without meaning to.

"Sit down. My sister can hear you perfectly well from a seated position," August immediately came to my defence and I gave her a grateful smile.

It was good to have her around again. I'd forgotten what a fire-cracker she could be at times.

Rudy lowered himself into his chair and moved it closer to Patrice, who gazed into the distance.

"What would I even do with money like that?" She asked.

"We'll figure it out, don't you worry about that!" Rudy said with a grin.

"You could take some time off. You're still at the nursing home, right?" Nick suggested.

Patrice nodded. "I like my work. And I like my home. Sure, I could buy some real fancy things with money like that, but do I really need those fancy things?"

"You know I've had my eye on the Lamborghini Gallardo. Santa never brings me one," Rudy said with a pointed look across at Nick.

"Rudy, please. We're not together."

"We're not divorced, though. That means what's yours is mine, right?"

Patrice groaned. "I don't know what to do. If Artie had been cut off by his son, it doesn't feel like the right thing for me to hand over the money and the business to Sprout."

"Listen, it's getting late, dear. There's really no rush to make a decision. Why don't you both spend the night here and things might seem fresher in the morning. Do you have overnight things?"

Patrice shook her head.

"I carry my things with me everywhere ever since she kicked me out," Rudy grumbled. "But don't worry, my darling. A few million pounds will help me get over that."

"Let me show you to your rooms. I'll have Gilbert find some things for you, Patrice. We always have spares of everything here."

"They really do. One of the first things I was told about was Mrs Claus' love for bringing in waifs and strays," I quipped to August.

"It looks like Nick isn't hating that habit right about now," she said.

I followed her gaze and saw that Nick - and his dimple - were smiling at me dreamily. I forced myself to look away before my stomach could flip... nope, there was no point. I was defenceless against his charm and good looks.

"I've been really excited to get to meet you, August. Did you find Candy Cane Hollow okay?" Nick asked.

"It was weird. I obviously got here okay but my memory is blanking on the journey. I'm probably just overexcited about getting to see my big sister!"

"And plan a ball," I said.

August grinned. "Can we get started on that tonight? I spent some time earlier drawing up some initial ideas and I think I have it all broken down into five main categories. Of course, you can disagree."

I laughed and shook my head. I would never disagree with August's organisational skills. She was a master at her craft.

The door opened and Rudy appeared, huge owl-like glasses covering the top half of his face.

"Did I leave my lavender sleep spray down here?"

"I don't think so. Nearly didn't recognise you with those specs on," Nick said with a smile.

"I'm as blind as a bat without them."

"You did a good job of hiding that earlier," I said.

"Oh! No, I wear contacts in the day. Glasses make me feel a bit too... erm... bookish."

I didn't know that there was such a thing as too bookish, so I raised my eyebrows and offered a smile.

"I'll probably get that laser eye surgery now we have some money to spend," Rudy said with a wink.

After he had departed, I stayed up for a while with August. I explained to her that the Winter Ball was one of the many highlights of the festive calendar in Candy Cane Hollow, and she grinned and rubbed her hands together with glee.

"I don't get to plan anything these days. This is going to be such a treat," she enthused.

"You mean you're not hosting your dinner soirees any more?" I asked.

August gave a slow smile. "They don't really fit in with having a baby around. My evenings are mainly focused on feeding and changing Jeb, then putting him to bed and praying he sleeps through the night."

"Sounds rough," I said. My years of medical school and residency had given me a pretty high tolerance for disturbed sleep, but August had always liked to get an undisturbed eight hours. As a minimum.

August's cheeks grew rosy. "But he's so amazing, Holly. I could just eat him. He's such a good baby."

I grinned. Nothing made me happier than seeing my sister so happy.

We spent a while longer chatting about her plans for the Ball, and I mainly sat back and nodded my agreement. She had thought of things I would never consider, and it was clear to see that under her direction, the Winter Ball would be incredible.

Finally, we began to yawn, and agreed to get ready for bed. I was excited about getting to share a bedroom with her again after all these years.

We changed into our pyjamas and climbed into the twin beds in our guest room. Outside, the snow was falling and August sat for a while gazing out at the fairytale scene beyond the window.

"I can't believe you live here," she murmured.

"Neither can I," I admitted, then I allowed my eyes to close and sleep to take me.

5

I was woken the next morning by August's alarm clock, which signalled that it was just after 6am.

"Erm, are you kidding me?"

"Sorry," August groaned as she threw the blankets off of her and got to her feet. I'd never seen someone wake up with such fierce determination. I snuggled back down under my blankets and attempted to get back to sleep.

There was no need for such an early hour to be experienced on a day when I was off work. I'd arranged for the doctor's surgery to be manned by a retired GP so that I could focus on August during her visit.

The peace was shattered by August's mummy voice and I opened my eyes to see her dialling in for a video call with Jeb.

"Hey baby! Mummy's here! I wuv you! Oh yes I do! Who is mummy's favourite teddy bear?! Of course it's you! Mwah, mwah, mwah, I wuv you sweet cheeks!"

Her tone changed back to her usual in control tones when her husband Tom appeared on screen. "Did you remember it's Rattle and Rhyme this morning? Don't miss it again because they have a very strict policy on non-attendance. Did you send the form back for swimming lessons? It's in the folder, of course. Did you remember to do the baby yoga exercises before bed last night?"

I realised that I had no chance of finding sleep again and stumbled out of bed and into the en suite. I could hear August continue to grill Tom and give him orders as I splashed my face with cold water.

My thoughts turned to Nick. He had acted strange the night before. I thought he'd stay up with August and me, but he'd done a pretty poor imitation yawn after Rudy popped back down, and went up to bed. Maybe he wanted to give us some uninterrupted sister time.

I returned to the bedroom when I thought it was safe to, and found August sitting on the bed in tears.

"Sis, what's wrong?"

She sniffled and shook her head. "He just looked so beautiful and I miss him so much."

"Oh, August! Do you want to go home?" I asked.

"No, no. I need to do this. I want to do this! It's just hard seeing his little face and not being able to pick him up and smother him in kisses. Man, hormones are a killer. Right. I need caffeine," she said, and made an effort to clear her features and look cheerful.

"Let's go," I said. "But be quiet. It's too early for Gilbert to be down there, and if he realises we've made ourselves drinks, we'll never hear the end of it."

Together, we crept downstairs slowly, listening out for any steps that creaked. We had done the same as children, attempting to listen to the secret conversations we imagined our parents to have after our bedtime. We'd never been caught, and I really hoped that we kept that record because I didn't want to have to deal with Gilbert if he found us.

I was more scared of that elf than I ever had been of my parents.

At the bottom of the stairs August almost trod on Snowy, who was curled up in a ball sleeping. Her soft purrs must have touched something maternal inside of August for she began to sniffle again, and I gave her a jab with my elbow to remind her to be quiet.

The commotion woke the cat, who weaved around and around August's legs.

"She really does like you," I said. Usually, Snowy was loyal only to Mrs Claus.

"Cute baby," August said as she bent and picked Snowy up. As soon as she did so, the cat jumped out of her arms and walked a few steps down the corridor, then stopped and looked back at us.

"I think she wants us to follow her," August said.

I raised an eyebrow. "To the food bowl, no doubt. Come on, we have to get in and out with our coffees before Gilbert wakes up."

"Look at her, she's trying to tell us something," August persisted.

I wondered why I had ever worried about August's reaction to Candy Cane Hollow. Not only had she taken the existence of the Claus family in her stride and made friends with talking reindeer, she also believed the cat was trying to communicate with us.

"Fine," I said. It was clear we weren't getting our coffee until August had followed Snowy wherever the cat was off to. Hopefully that wouldn't be to her litter box.

The little cat lead us to the den and scratched at the oak door.

"Stop that! Mrs Claus might swap you for a dog," I murmured as I pushed the door open.

I didn't have a second to see what Snowy was trying to tell us, because August chose that moment to blow our cover with the loudest scream I'd ever heard in my life.

I tried to clamp my hand over her mouth but she fought me like a wildcat, and by the time she'd stopped making that awful noise, the staircase was full of the other occupants of Claus Cottage.

Gilbert was at the front of the pack, a tartan dressing gown protecting his modesty. He eyed us suspiciously. "What are you two doing down here?"

I gave a nervous laugh. "Oh, nothing! Just had some trouble sleeping."

"Well, that scream sure helped, I'll bet," he quipped. His gaze travelled across to the kitchen and I felt grateful that I could honestly say we hadn't been in there.

"Yeah. Sorry about that. I don't know what came over her," I said.

August stared off into space as if in a daze. Her mouth was still open from the screaming fit, and her eyes were as wide as saucers.

"Whatever happened, dear?" Mrs Claus asked as she squeezed past Gilbert and approached us. When August gave no answer, Mrs Claus made to push open the door to the den.

"No!" August exclaimed, but it was too late.

Mrs Claus had the door open and we all looked in. August began to scream again.

There, on the floor, was the lifeless figure of Rudy the elf.

6

As the notes of Last Christmas played out, I knew that Wiggles was approaching and felt some relief. The police would get everything cleared up, I hoped.

Wiggles let himself in and ducked his head as he offered condolences to everyone. We had gathered in the grand dining room and Gilbert had made hot chocolates for everyone.

"Do we have next of kin here?" Wiggles asked the group.

Patrice reluctantly raised her hand. "I'm his wife. We were separated, but not divorced."

"I'm sorry for your loss," Wiggles said.

"Wiggles, I'm sure you're aware, but there's the funeral of Artie Rumples today. Sprout here is his son. There won't be any issues with attending that, I hope?" Mrs Claus asked. As always, she was thinking of someone other than herself.

Wiggles glanced across at Sprout. "This here is a murder investigation. I'll be as quick as I can, but these things take time. I'll need to speak to you before you go to the funeral."

"Yes, sir," Sprout said and rose from his seat at the table.

"Not now. I need to see the body first. Holly, can I borrow you?"

I nodded and downed my hot chocolate before standing up. Gilbert took it as a personal affront when his drinks went to waste.

I followed Wiggles into the den and looked anywhere but at the carpet, where Rudy lay. One of his arms was stretched out towards a chair, as if he'd been attempting to reach for something in his last moments. I swallowed and tried to get that image out of my head.

"You know this fellow?" Wiggles asked as he stood over the body and made a rudimentary sketch of its positioning.

I shook my head. "He turned up here last night. He seemed to have followed Patrice and she wasn't too happy about it."

"I'm not surprised," Wiggles said as he pulled out his smartphone and snapped some photographs, first of Rudy and then of the whole room.

"You knew him?"

"He's got a record a mile long. All for the same thing, too. If he'd been a bit more inventive, he might have got away with some of it but the elf just had a thing for counterfeit tickets," Wiggles explained as he pulled a tape measure from his pocket and noted down measurements.

"Counterfeit tickets?"

"He hawked those things at every event going. I don't understand why people carried on buying from him. Patrice was right to kick him out, if you ask me. What were they doing here, anyway?"

"Erm. I don't know if it's my place to say," I answered warily. Patrice seemed so conflicted about Artie's Will, I didn't know if she'd want the news sharing with other people.

"Fine, fine. I'll ask her myself. It's unusual for her to get a day off work, though," Wiggles murmured, more to himself than me.

"She came to Mrs Claus asking for her help with something. I'd prefer to say no more because it's not my news to share," I said.

"Fair enough. Hmm, that's interesting," Wiggles murmured as he leaned in close to the dead elf's face.

I followed his gaze and saw that Rudy's eyes were completely red, as if a bloodshot patch had taken over his whole eyeball.

"That doesn't look good," I said.

"You ever seen anything like that before, doc?"

I leaned in closer. The whole eyeball was red and looked awfully sore. "Bloodshot eyes happen when the blood vessels burst. That can happen for any number of reasons. Even something as simple as a sneeze. But I've never seen whole eyeballs look like that."

"Me either. It's not like the strangulation case I saw a few years ago."

"There's been a strangulation here?" I asked in surprise.

Wiggles shrugged. "Poor guy slipped off a stepladder while putting up some Christmas lights. The wire got wrapped around his..."

"Gosh. What a way to go," I murmured. "But, no, this isn't strangulation. When that happens, the eyes tend to go black. Or there can be blood in them. This almost looks like an allergic reaction, which is weird."

"It's strange, indeed. I don't understand how anyone could let someone touch their eyes. Gives me the creeps!" Wiggles said as a shudder pulsed through the length of his body.

"Me too. Hey, Rudy told me last night that he's blind as a bat without his glasses on. Does he have his contact lenses in?"

Wiggles looked up at me, then stood to make space for me to get in closer. "You have a look. See what you think."

I leaned in and saw the ring of contact lenses around his pupils. "Yep, he's wearing them. So he would have seen whatever happened to him. What are you thinking? Some kind of natural death? A sudden disease?"

"You'd be the expert on that, not me," Wiggles said.

I pursed my lips and considered my medical training. I knew a lot about a lot of illnesses, but my training had never focused on the possibility of me living in a frozen tundra. There were a lot of foul things that could happen to the body in such extreme weather.

"I'd have to do some research," I admitted.

"Please do. I don't want to jump to conclusions here, but something doesn't sit right with me. I'm going to speak to everyone here, just in case Rudy's death wasn't natural."

**

As Wiggles spoke to everyone present, August and I retreated to our guest room and continued working on the Winter Ball plans. August's plans had grown even more extensive and elaborate overnight and I felt grateful that the Ball was the next day so she couldn't get even more carried away.

The initial plans rolled over from year to year, but this year would be the first time I was going to put my own personal stamp on the event. It was a big moment, and I was glad August was by my side for it.

We were disturbed from our planning by a knock on the door. I shouted for the person to come in, and Patrice stood in the doorway.

"S-s-sorry to interrupt. Can I c-c-come in?"

"Oh! Sure! Don't mind the mess, we're planning to take over the world," I joked as I hastily moved piles of paper and created a space for Patrice to sit on one of the beds.

"How are you doing?" August asked.

Patrice shrugged. "I wanted rid of him for a long time, and now he's really gone. But, still, he was my husband."

"It sounds complicated."

"If only he'd listened to me and not followed me over here," she said.

"What do you mean?" I asked.

"Then he wouldn't have got killed!" She exclaimed, then began to cry.

"You think he was murdered?" I asked.

"W-w-well, what else could it be? Wiggles doesn't come over every time a person dies. And Rudy was in good health. Better than he deserved."

"He didn't have any health issues you know of?"

"None. He sailed through his annual Well Elf checks and never stopped boasting about it. Surely, someone killed him?"

"Maybe," I admitted. "Do you have any idea who could have hurt him?"

Patrice's upper lip began to wobble. "They'll think it was me, won't they?"

"Probably," August said. I jabbed her with my elbow again. I'd forgotten how black and white she could be. She gave a yelp and looked at me. "What? There's no point telling Patrice she's wrong. Rudy followed her all this way and he seemed hell bent on getting that inheritance money."

Patrice closed her eyes and began to sway back and forth on the bed. "I never wanted money. Sure, an extra hundred or two would be nice. The bills can be a stretch at times. But I never in my life imagined the kind of money Mr Artie left me."

"Maybe we need to get to the bottom of why Artie left the money to you. That could be connected to the murder," I said. "If there was a murder."

"There was. I'm sure of it," Patrice said.

I didn't want to tell her, but even the fact that she was talking about murder was suspicious. Surely the only person who knew if there had been a murder at this stage was the killer.

"Think back really hard. You must have met Artie at some point?" August prompted.

Patrice bit her lip and shook her head. "I would have remembered. My life is very predictable. I go to work and I go home. I rarely leave Mistletoe Moor."

"So Artie must have had some connection with your job?"

Patrice shook her head. "I'm an Elf Care Assistant at the Jingle Bells Nursing Home. The closest we've ever come to Artie is his Festive Feast meals. Our patients really enjoy them."

"Maybe he left it to you because the nursing home has been such a good customer?" August suggested.

"I don't do any of the ordering. I'm not in the office, I'm actually out there with patients, caring for them through the day and night."

"That's hard work," I said. Although I was a GP, I'd spent enough time in hospital settings and I knew that care assistants often did the majority of the grunt work. Those jobs were physically demanding and emotionally draining. It took a special kind of person - or elf - to do it.

Patrice shrugged. "As Gilbert's alluded to, I didn't concentrate too well in school. My options were limited. But I joined Jingle Bells right out of school and I've been there ever since. I love what I do."

"And you're sure Artie's never visited? He hasn't ever delivered the meals himself or popped by to say hello to the patients?" I asked.

Patrice shook her head. "Not to my knowledge but it is possible. I don't know if I'd have recognised him. The whole Moor knows the rumours about him living out in a shack, surviving on a pittance because of a broken heart, but he didn't really court the media. I never saw a photo of him."

"Let me find one," I said. I pulled out my smart phone and searched for Artie. To my surprise, there were shockingly few images of the eccentric millionaire. There were a couple of blurry shots that purported to be Artie in the middle of Mistletoe Moor, dashing back to his shack, and there was a photo of a much younger Artie, a crying baby Sprout on his knee.

Finally, I found a headshot on the Festive Feast website, accompanying an obituary notice. In the image, Artie looked to be around seventy years old. He was handsome in a refined way, and something about the image suggested to me that Artie looked nothing like that in his day to day life.

Still it was the best I could find. I held the image up to Patrice and she leaned in and studied it. Eventually she shook her head.

"I guess I could have seen him. But even if I did, what does that prove? The man was still a stranger to me even if I walked by him in the street once or twice. He had no reason to leave his fortune to me and I don't know if I can accept it. Sprout says he wasn't in his right mind! How can I deprive a son of his father's empire?"

"You don't have to decide that now," August soothed. "Today is Artie's funeral. The money is going to be the last thing on Sprout's mind. He'll just want to see his dad receive a good send off."

"If you say so," Patrice said, unconvinced.

"I do. Are you planning on attending the funeral?"

Patrice groaned. "I don't know what to do for the best. I feel like I should show my respects, but won't it upset Sprout to see me there?"

"We'll go with you," I volunteered.

August frowned.

"What?"

"I didn't pack any clothes appropriate for a funeral," she said.

"Neither did I," Patrice said.

7

I managed to find funeral appropriate clothes for August and
Patrice, and the three of us travelled across to the church in one
of the older sleighs. Mrs Claus and Father Christmas had travelled over with Sprout and Brandy in one of the ceremonial sleighs.

The reindeer were quiet, given the occasion. They had a surprisingly high level of emotional intelligence. Even Betty resisted asking
August for another spritz of perfume.

We pulled in to the church's car park, and the number of cars and
sleighs was a reflection of Artie's reputation. He had been an eccentric, but his company had created many jobs. His meals had given
those less able to cook the opportunity to enjoy a full Christmas
dinner as often as they liked.

The church was full to the rafters and buzzing with the whispered
conversations of the mourners. Sprout and Brandy were up front,
with Mrs Claus and Father Christmas right beside them. I watched as
Mrs Claus pulled a tissue from her handbag and dabbed at her eyes.

My mind was skittish as the vicar began the ceremony. I
wondered whether Mrs Claus was happy that her eulogy speech was
ready, and I also couldn't take my mind off Rudy.

Had he died of natural causes? Or had he been killed?

I thought back to his red eyes and searched my mind for any medical cases I had seen that were similar, but came up blank.

All I could think time and time again was that it looked like an allergic reaction. But how could eyeballs have an allergic reaction?

I gasped, and judging by August's reaction, I wasn't as quiet as I'd hoped.

"What is it?" she whispered. A couple of mourners in the row in front of us turned and pursed their lips at us disapprovingly.

"I'll tell you later," I replied, keeping my voice as low as I could.

I did my best to stay focused on the funeral. I certainly didn't want to disrespect Artie.

After prayers, hymns and the handing out of a Festive Feast voucher to each mourner, it was time for Mrs Claus to read out her eulogy. She walked across the stage with dignity and grace and I wondered if I would ever be as poised as she was.

When she reached the podium, she took a moment to look out at the crowd. She had a way of making each person feel as if she had looked right at them, and after her quick look, everyone in the pews gazed at her lovingly.

"First of all, I want to say how wonderful it is to see so many of you here to celebrate the life of our dear friend, Artichoke Rumples. You will have known him as Artie, or as the creator of our beloved Festive Feast meals, or perhaps as an eccentric man who kept himself to himself. Artie was all of those things, and more. He was a widower, having lost his dear wife too many years ago. I'm sure you'll join me in celebrating their heavenly reunion now," Mrs Claus said, then paused.

A soft murmur passed through the church. "Hallelujah."

"Artie was also a father. His son Sprout is here today, and may he feel carried by the love and support we are all here to provide. Artie was a loyal friend, although his shyness didn't allow him to make friends easily. He shied away from any kind of fuss. Even as his business grew, he was happy remaining in the small home he had always lived in, and he refused any kind of special treatment or luxuries. He lived a regular life, and he was happy."

"He sounds wonderful," Patrice whispered beside me. It wasn't clear whether she'd even intended me to hear her words, but I reached over and took her hand in mine.

"I'd like to ask you each to spend a moment remembering him. Please close your eyes and take a minute to think of our friend Artie," Mrs Claus asked. She closed her eyes and held on to the lectern to steady herself.

I closed my own eyes and Patrice allowed her hand to slip free of mine. I opened my eye a fraction and saw that she held her hands together, as if she was praying. Of course. She had no memories of Artie. A prayer was a wonderful idea.

I closed my eyes and mimicked the gesture she was making, then said a silent prayer. I prayed that Artie had been reunited with his wife, and that he was returned to full health for the afterlife. I then prayed that Sprout would find peace, and that Patrice would be given the strength to use her unexpected inheritance for good.

"Artie. We were blessed to know you, blessed to call you a member of our community, and blessed by your business skills. We hope you rest in peace. Amen," Mrs Claus said. Her voice wobbled slightly to indicate the emotion she was feeling, but otherwise she was as slick a presenter as any I'd ever seen. In fact, even the wobble added to how impressive she was.

"Amen," I murmured.

I opened my eyes and glanced at August, who was dabbing at her eyes with a tissue. She turned to me and I saw that barely a speck of her mascara was still attached to her lashes.

"Are you okay?" I asked.

She nodded, then blew her nose into the tissue, which attracted more disapproving looks. "Funerals always get to me. I'm an emotional mess since having Jeb."

"Motherhood will do that to you," I teased, although I had no idea.

She shook her head. "I'm terrible. I should have warned you before I came."

"I should have warned you. I bet you didn't expect your visit here to include a funeral and a murder."

"Please be quiet," the lady sat in front of me turned around and said. She wore a deep scowl on her face.

My cheeks flushed. "Sorry."

Feeling well and truly told off, and for a good reason, I didn't even want to look at August. It was easy to forget that we could be a bad influence on each other. We just got so giddy to chat to each other, it was hard to control. But we were at a funeral, and I was determined not to cause Mrs Claus any embarrassment.

I glanced to my left to see how Patrice was holding up, and realised with a start that she was gone.

8

The rest of the funeral went quickly and without a hitch. August and I didn't so much as glance at each other, never mind speak, until we were off the church grounds completely.

We decided to travel to the Festival Hall on foot. It was cold, as always, but it wasn't snowing, and the fresh snowfall from the morning meant that the paths were nice and fluffy instead of wet and icy.

"I wonder where Patrice went," I murmured as we closed the churchyard gate behind us with a creak.

"Maybe she struggled with the emotion of it all like me," August said with a smile as she kicked some snow.

"Maybe. I figured she'd say bye though," I said as we fell into a comfortable walking pace and headed in the direction of the Festival Hall.

"And risk the wrath of the ladies in front of us?" August asked with a giggle. I allowed myself a smile.

"I can't believe we got told off for talking. It was like being back in school assembly."

"Gosh! I haven't thought of assembly in a long time! Do you

remember how we had to sit on the floor? That shiny wooden floor? It was so slippy. And the teachers crammed us all in there. Until you got to the last year and then you could sit at the back on a bench."

"I thought I'd reached the big time when I could sit on a bench," I admitted.

"Right?!" My sister asked with a laugh.

"I never could have guessed then that we'd be in Candy Cane Hollow planning a Winter Ball together!"

"Me either. This place is so cool, Holly. You know what I think is odd?"

"The talking reindeer?"

She shook her head. "Oh no. They're cute!"

"The fact that my boyfriend is Santa?"

August raised an eyebrow. "Mr Hunkalicious can be whoever he wants as long as he treats my big sister well!"

"Well if those two things don't strike you as odd, I give up."

"Why didn't Artie have a wake?"

I stopped and looked at her. "Hmm. That's a good question. I hadn't thought about it."

"It's just... he had all that money. He seems like a pretty big person around town. You'd think there would be some kind of get together after the funeral."

"But who would organise that? I heard Sprout say that the funeral was all prepaid."

"It would be his next of kin, right?" August asked as we continued trudging through the snow.

"I guess. So that would be Sprout."

"And they were estranged, right?"

I nodded. "That's what I've heard. But Sprout was right there at the funeral. I'll bet he regrets whatever they fell out about. It's easy to stay angry but then when someone dies, that has to change everything. I'll bet he wishes things had been different."

"Wouldn't a wake be a good step towards that?" August asked.

"I guess. Where would the money come from, though? Sprout hasn't inherited anything, so he'd have to pay for it himself."

"You don't think he would?"

I considered the question, and Sprout's desperation to get what he considered to be his inheritance. "I wonder if he couldn't afford it."

"Really? Oh. Wow... that's rough," August said.

I shrugged. "I could be wrong. He doesn't look poor in that big fur coat. Anyway, here we are. Welcome to the Festival Hall!"

August gasped as she took in the building in front of us. It was circular and featured full height windows the whole way around. The pillars that separated the glass and provided the structural support were decorated with heavy poinsettia garlands, and the lawn in front of the Hall featured snow sculptures of animals. The collection of deer, rabbits and birds looked right out of a Disney movie.

"This is incredible," August finally managed to speak.

I grinned and squeezed her arm. "And tomorrow it will be the venue for the most fantastic Winter Ball ever seen. I can't wait to be there with you, dancing the night away. I've been working on my moves for weeks, you know."

August took in the space the way an architect would, or an interior designer. Someone with a more visual eye than mine, in any event.

She murmured and smiled to herself as she took in the shape of the room, the space for the grand ballroom dance floor, the stage where Michael Bauble would perform.

"So what exactly is there left to plan?" She asked when she had finished her assessment.

"We have to, erm, get the room ready? The entertainer is booked, the food is ordered, it's really just our job to make this space look festive," I explained.

The Winter Ball would be the first event I had prepared without Mrs Claus leading the way. She had been on hand, of course, to help when needed, but she was also pushing me to do more and more on my own. It had been nerve-racking, until August announced her visit, and I realised that she could help me get everything ready.

Mrs Claus had approved of that plan and encouraged me to put my own stamp on the event. Michael Bauble was a familiar performer, often starring at Candy Cane Hollow events, so I had booked him as soon as the date had been confirmed. I knew that the guests would look forward to hearing him again, and I'd even persuaded him to include a couple of new songs in his line-up.

Organising all of those practical things had been a little over-whelming, but also doable. I knew how to work my way through a task list of errands in a pretty efficient way, and Mrs Claus had been there to guide me when necessary.

But deciding on a colour scheme for the room? Decorating the space? Those things were so far out of my comfort zone, I didn't know where to begin.

Luckily, my baby sister had a design eye to kill for. Every room in her cottage home was immaculate and like something out of a magazine.

"Okay. So we need to dress the space. It's a good size," she murmured.

"Dress the space?" I repeated.

"Yep. Think of it as if the room is a blank canvas. It has a lot of potential, and it's our job to bring that to life. Now, you mentioned there are lots of props we can use?"

"Sure, I'll show you," I said with a nod. I lead the way to the storage area, which was almost as big as the ballroom itself. August gasped with delight as she took in the sight of the wreaths, garlands, artificial Christmas trees, tinsel, decorations, lights, and life-size figures of snowmen, reindeer and more.

"Gosh," August said. She looked a little stunned as she surveyed the space.

"We also have help available. There's several staff here who will lend a hand carrying things and setting things out for us."

"That's good to hear. Some of those things look heavy. And deli-cate," she said as she picked up a box filled with antique glass snowflake ornaments.

"Those have belonged to the Claus family for generations," I said with a swell of pride. It was just like Mrs Claus to leave her family's valuables in the storage room for anyone to use when needed. That woman's generosity had no end.

"They're incredible. All unique, as well," August said as she studied them.

"Well, they say every snowflake is, so the decorations should be too," I said with a grin. Mrs Claus had explained the same thing to me when I'd first noticed them, and it felt like a rite of passage to explain the same to my sister.

"We need a colour scheme to begin with," August said as she returned the box to the floor. "Do you have any ideas?"

I shrugged. "You're better at those details than I am."

"I was thinking of gold and white. We could do the more traditional red and green, that would look great too, but I think if we do heavy white with gold accents, it will reflect the snow outside. What do you think?"

I gazed at August as if she had spoken to me in a language I didn't understand, because basically she had. "I can't believe you can do that, look at a space and see how the colours will come together. It's so cool."

August gave a shy smile. "We all have our different talents. I can't treat an infection like you do for your patients."

"That's more the medication than me," I said.

"Yes, and you know which medication and how much. Being a doctor is amazing, don't put yourself down," August scolded.

"Okay. I won't. So, white and gold. We have lots of white pine garlands, did you spot them already?"

August shook her head and I rummaged around until I found what I was looking for. The garlands were artificial, but such high quality they looked - and even smelled - like real pine. They were thick, and heavy, and came with several subtle clips built in where decorations could be added.

"Those are perfect. We can clip in some gold stars or pinecones to add to the appearance. Do you think we can get some ladders and fix these around the perimeter of the ceiling?"

I nodded. "Definitely. There's a caretaker on site, he'll be happy to give a hand."

"If there's enough, we can wrap them around the pillars by the entrance too. That's going to need a steady hand as we need the spacing to be the same. I'll probably just do that myself."

"And what can I do?" I asked.

August surveyed the space and her eyes landed on the human-size snowman figures. "How about these guys by the door as if they're welcoming people in?"

I laughed. "Great idea! These statues actually aren't heavy, I can move them."

"Are you sure? The last thing you want is to injure yourself and have to miss the Winter Ball after all of your hard work."

"I'll be fine. I'll ask for help if I need to."

"Okay. Good. We need something we can use as centre pieces for each table as well. Actually, ooh! Look at these!" August exclaimed as she reached out and picked up a small, empty goldfish bowl.

"What are you thinking?" I asked.

"If we can give these a quick clean, I think they'll work great. We can fill them with beads, or put a fake candle in each one. Lots of options!"

I shook my head happily. My sister was the perfect person to do this with me!

We each got to work, and filled a happy afternoon setting things up. By the time we called it a day, the space was transformed. There was still work to do, but already it was taking shape and I knew that the end result would be breathtaking.

Mrs Claus was going to be pleased with our efforts, and that made me happy. She had been so kind to trust me with such a responsibility, and I didn't want to let her down.

9

By the time we returned to Claus Cottage, we were exhausted and our clothes were dusty. Gilbert crinkled his nose as we stood in the hallway taking off our winter boots.

"And you two can get upstairs to the shower before you think of traipsing into my kitchen!" He commanded as he waved a wooden spoon in our general direction without getting too close to us.

We knew better than to argue and made our way upstairs, where I insisted that August take the first shower. While she was in there, I noticed her phone screen light up and glanced at it in case it was an urgent phone call.

It was a message from her husband, Tom, and the full text appeared on the screen.

Meeting didn't go well babe. Will need to chat when you're home. :-(

My cheeks flushed as I realised that I had read something personal that wasn't intended for my eyes. August hadn't mentioned anything about a meeting. In fact, she'd barely mentioned Tom since she'd arrived. Was she having problems in her marriage? It wouldn't be surprising if she was, they were a busy couple with a young child.

But, no. It wasn't my place to speculate. I busied myself by opening the wardrobe and picking out a fresh change of clothes.

I hadn't spoken to Nick for a while and decided to give him a call, but his phone rang out and the voicemail kicked in. I didn't leave a message. I didn't have a message... I just felt like hearing his voice. He had been working crazy hours recently, which was a part of the job that would never change. I knew that and accepted it. A career in medicine came with its own intense working schedule at times. But I missed him.

Never mind. He would call me back when he could.

August emerged from the shower, all squeaky clean and refreshed, and I went and got myself cleaned up.

By the time we made our way downstairs, the house was quieter than I'd expect. Gilbert served us a portion of his signature chicken soup and we ate it hungrily, as if we had been starved for days.

"Are you still hungry?"

"Erm, a little," August admitted. She didn't realise how fragile the elf's ego was, and I braced myself for him to panic that his food was inadequate, but to my surprised he grinned at us maniacally.

"Excellent! Stay right there. Cheese and onion toasties coming right up!" Gilbert exclaimed, and within moments half a toasted sandwich was placed in front of each of us.

"Oh, wow. Thanks, Gilbert," I said. August and I devoured our second course and sat back, satisfied.

"You're more than welcome. People who turn up when expected and eat are always welcome in my kitchen, you know that!"

"Gilbert, dear, you're not still talking about poor Patrice, are you?" Mrs Claus' voice came from the hallway. She spotted August and me and grinned. "Oh! Hello, dears! I didn't hear you two get back."

"What's happening with Patrice?" I asked.

"It's nothing, dear."

"I'll tell you exactly what's going on with that no-good elf. She had a dinner date right here, and your guess is as good as mine about where she is. I can tell you where she isn't! She isn't here, where she should be!"

August and I glanced at each other. "Have you just given us Patrice's dinner?"

"What was I meant to do, save it for whenever she decides to wander in here?"

"It's no trouble, dears. Gilbert can make another toastie when she gets home," Mrs Claus said.

Gilbert opened his mouth but no words came out. Mrs Claus had caught him in a perfect, cunning trap. He wanted to object, of course he did, but he was also the proudest elf I knew, and making a toastie wasn't beyond him. So he couldn't moan. He couldn't say anything.

He just stood before us, his mouth wide open, as he realised that he had been caught in the domestic version of check mate.

"Do close your mouth, dear," Mrs Claus said with a smile.

"Has Patrice not come back since the funeral?" I asked.

Mrs Claus shook her head. "I looked for her at the end of the service but she was nowhere around. I'm sure she's just getting some air."

"It's freezing out there," August protested.

"Ah, not for a local. It's surprising how quickly you can adapt to the weather," Mrs Claus said with a wink.

"She's right. But still, it's worrying that she's out there on her own. She is coming back, right? I mean, she doesn't live here. Maybe she's gone back to her home."

Gilbert rolled his eyes. "I was cleaning her guest room earlier and think it's fairly safe to say she's planning on returning."

"Oh. What makes you say that?"

"Firstly, she didn't make her bed this morning. Second, she left her socks on the floor. And third, there's a glass of water on the bedside table," Gilbert listed the catalogue of reasons on his fingers.

"Well, that's settled. I'm sure she'll be back when she's ready."

We were interrupted by a knock at the door, and there was an unspoken battle to see who could get to it quickest. Mrs Claus was in the lead but Gilbert sprinted down the hallway and got ahead of her.

He answered the door and we all gazed at the man who stood on the doorstep in a full suit, a briefcase in his hand.

"Are Mr and Mrs Rumples in? It's Bertram Smythe to see them," he asked. He had the voice of wealth; a rich, smooth voice that suggested a life of abundance and luxury. A life of hearing only yes.

"Mr and Mrs... oh. Sprout and his wife? They have their visitors turn up unannounced now, do they? Is that the point we're at with house guest manners?" Gilbert muttered.

"Do come in, dear," Mrs Claus said, and Bertram Smythe moved forward with such confidence that Gilbert had to duck to one side before he was ploughed over.

"I'll fetch them, shall I?" Gilbert mumbled, but nobody answered, and he trudged up the stairs in a way that made it obvious he was unhappy about the whole thing.

Mrs Claus showed Bertram Smythe into the den, and August and I followed, our curiosity making it impossible for us to do anything else.

Bertram Smythe's name was familiar, but I couldn't place where I had heard or seen it. He was dressed in a manner that was so flashy it seemed entirely out of place in Candy Cane Hollow. He looked like an investment banker, or a lawyer, or even a crook. I realised that there was every chance my thoughts were being reflected in the expression on my face, and made the effort to neutralise my gaze.

Sprout burst into the room, Brandy a few steps behind him. While Sprout zoned straight in on Bertram Smythe, Brandy flushed and gave August and me apologetic glances.

"What's the meaning of this, Smythe? You know the old man was losing his marbles!" Sprout bellowed. Luckily, he was so annoyed he didn't seem to even notice August and me sitting in the corner, never mind object to us being present.

"I know no such thing, Sprout. It's good to see you, by the way. And you're very welcome for this home visit. Is it too much to ask for a drink before we get into the shouting match?"

Sprout huffed, turned and surveyed the room as if looking for anyone who could make a drink, not supposing for a second that he should do it himself.

"I'll be happy to make drinks," Gilbert said in a tone that revealed he was anything but.

"We do appreciate you coming out like this, honestly. It's just... emotions are high," Brandy explained. She had the expression of a long-suffering woman who was used to apologising for the man in her life.

"Quite. But I must reiterate, I'm here as a favour to your father, Mr Rumples. There is simply nothing more to say on the matter," Bertram said with a grimace.

"Oh, come on, Bertie. There's always a loophole," Sprout said as an affable grin spread across his face.

"There's no such thing. And it would do you well to remember who you're speaking to. I know you've seen me ever since you were a young boy, but I was your father's lawyer and I remain instructed to ensure his wishes are carried out."

"And his wishes would be for his only son and heir to be taken care of. You know that! If he was thinking properly..." Sprout said with a shrug.

"He was thinking properly, I can assure you of that. If I'd had any doubt, I'd have refused to take instructions and would have reported the matter to the Bar-Humbug Council myself."

"Everyone says he lost his way over the last few years. Never leaving that dreadful shack..."

"That dreadful shack was his lifelong home, and a perfectly good one. You grew up there and managed to come out okay," Bertram said with a sniff as Gilbert entered the room and placed hot chocolates in front of everyone.

"Thank you," Brandy said with a meek smile.

"But he became reclusive! He never saw anyone!"

"Who should he have seen, Mr Rumples? When his only son was refusing any contact with him?"

Sprout glared at the solicitor. "What do you know about it?"

"A good deal more than I'd like to. Now, I'll say it again. My instructions have always been to act in your father's best wishes. Not yours! I'm here as a courtesy, and I won't even bill you for this time. But you have to understand that you took the decision to cut yourself off from your father, and you can't be surprised that his Will reflects that reality."

"I'm still his blood! Listen, Bertie, I don't want to have to drag this thing through the Bah-Humbug Council, but it's obvious to me that this Will can't stand. Did father even know that elf?!"

"You mean the beneficiary?" Bertram asked, and I realised that he was being vague about mentioning Patrice's identity. Did he fear that Sprout could take matters into his own hands and hurt her? Or was he just bound by client confidentiality?

"Of course I mean the so-called beneficiary. She says she never even met the old man. You're telling me he picked a name at random to leave his entire estate to, and that's legit?"

"I'm telling you that a person can dispose of their estate entirely as they see fit, as long as they're of sound mind and not being placed under duress. Whether she was your father's best friend, a lover or a complete stranger makes no difference at all."

"A lover?" Sprout asked, his eyes wide. Suddenly his mouth formed a leering, menacing grin. "That's it! She's far too young for him, and she even works with old folk. I bet she's a professional con woman! Yes, that's it. I bet old Artie was just the latest in a line of gullible old fools!"

"Enough!" Mrs Claus ordered from the doorway.

We all turned to look at her, stunned to hear her give such a command. She stood firm, her expression impossible to read.

"I will not have your father disrespected, Sprout, dear. Not in Claus Cottage. Not within my hearing. Now, I understand that emotions are high, but you'll proceed with respect. Thank you," she said, her voice returned to her normal, calm tones, and then she turned and left the room.

"Well said," Bertram mumbled as he sniffed and took a long sip of his hot chocolate.

"Sprout doesn't mean any disrespect, sir. It's just... we were counting on that money," Brandy said, her voice high and trembling.

Sprout glared at her. "I'll handle this."

She gave a nod and swallowed, then turned her attention on her hot chocolate as if something about it was fascinating.

"What is it? Gambling again?" Bertram asked.

Sprout rolled his eyes. "He told you? Oh, I bet he told you everything. Or his side, at least. I'm not a gambler, Bertie. I'm an investor. I back businesses and look for opportunities. Some of them turn out well, others don't. It's just a losing run right now. I'm a little overextended financially."

"You've always managed to bounce back," Bertram said.

"And I will now. But let's just say I was expecting my inheritance to come through soon."

Bertram raised a single eyebrow. "You were? How so?"

Sprout laughed. "The old man was getting on."

"He was as fit as a prize reindeer," Bertram said.

"But still. The grim reaper comes for us all eventually."

"There was nothing to suggest your father's passing was imminent. No illness, no decline. His heart gave out with no warning. If you've got yourself in a mess, boy, I'm afraid that's your problem."

Sprout fixed a pleasant smile to his face and somehow that was more chilling than his glares. "I'm saying there wouldn't be a problem if that elf hadn't somehow got him to change his Will."

"You can't honestly believe that your father was conned by her? He was the brightest bauble on the tree. There was nothing that slipped by him."

"We'll have to let the courts decide what's right. I'll need a copy of all of his papers," Sprout said.

"You know I can't release anything to you without a court order, and the courts don't like to involve themselves in a gentleman's personal affairs. I really am sorry, Sprout. I always hoped the two of you would reconcile. I really did."

Sprout scoffed. "Oh, yeah? I bet you were taking more than your fair share of money from the old man. It did you good not having me involved! I'll be getting that court order and I'll be checking all of your bills. Don't you think I won't!"

"Honey..." Brandy murmured, but her husband didn't appear to hear her.

Bertram downed the rest of his hot chocolate, wiped his mouth, and rose to his feet. He met Sprout's gaze and gave a nod. "I'll be going now. Goodbye, and good luck to you both, Mr and Mrs Rumples. I'll see myself out."

"Not in my home, you won't!" Gilbert's nasally voice came from the hallway, and he ushered the solicitor out of the room.

Sprout huffed and glared at his wife, who appeared to shrink in her chair.

"Why did you mention the money?"

"I just thought he'd understand why it mattered if we told him..." she said.

"It's not his business! I've told you I'll sort it before March and I will, alright?!"

Brandy glanced down and nodded.

Sprout dropped to his knees before her and clasped her hands in his. "Listen to me. Everything is going to be fine. Do you trust me?"

She nodded. "Of course."

"Good," he said, and he placed a hand on her stomach.

The tender moment was distracted by a shriek as the front door opened.

"What has happened to you? Look at this mess! I've just mopped the floor and now it needs doing again. As if I have nothing better to do! As if it's my job..." Gilbert ranted.

We all dashed to the hallway and there, covered in blood, was Patrice.

10

I managed to check Patrice over and declare that she was physically okay. Blood was often deceptive. She had a cut to her head, and it had bled for some time, but the blood had been diluted by the snow on the ground when she'd collapsed, and that had got all over her clothes.

We got her changed and wrapped up under a blanket, convinced Gilbert to stop mopping for a moment and make a hot chocolate, and waited until she was ready to explain.

"I went to the cemetery," she said, her voice shaky.

"What for, dear?" Mrs Claus asked.

Patrice frowned. "It will sound morbid."

"You can trust us," I said, and gave her hand a squeeze, partly to support her but also to check her body temperature. She was warming up nicely.

"So many of my patients, from the nursing home, have passed. I often go to the cemetery and just feel them with me. It's my safe place, I guess. Or at least, it used to be."

"Can you tell us what happened? Did you trip?"

Patrice shook her head and began to cry. "Someone hit me."

"No!" August gasped.

"I heard somebody walking behind me but I didn't think anything of it. I'm not the only one allowed in the graveyard, after all. The next thing I knew, something hit me and I fell to the ground."

"Did you get a look at him?" Sprout asked from across the room.

Before Patrice could answer, I stood up. "Let's not discuss this any more until Wiggles arrives. He'll need to take a full statement from you. I'll call him now."

I phoned the police officer and could tell that he was already in his car because Last Christmas played out in the background. He assured me that he was parked up enjoying a late lunch of a turkey sausage roll, and would be with us within minutes.

True to his word, just a minute or two later, we heard the smooth voice of George Michael belting out as Wiggles approached.

I let him in and found him accompanied by a man who looked like a walrus. He was huge, rotund and displayed a most excellent amount of facial hair.

"This is Cornelius. He's helping me out on a case we were doing a stake out for," Wiggles introduced.

I shook the man's hand and as he began to laugh, his jowls wobbled. "Sadly, it's a stake out and not a trip out for steak!"

"Good one!" Wiggles said with a giggle, then remembered the reason for their call and adopted a more sombre expression. "Now, Holly, you said it was urgent?"

I pulled the door of the den closed and lowered my voice. "Patrice has been attacked in the cemetery."

Wiggles scrunched up his face as if he didn't understand what I was saying.

"By a spirit?" Cornelius asked.

I blinked at him. "What? No. By a person... an alive person."

Cornelius grinned. "Phew! That's a relief. Spirits can be tricky to catch. Not to mention to apprehend. Or does that mean the same as catch? Apprehend. Let me see... Latin, if I'm right, and I've not been wrong on etymology since 1992. Don't ask! That's quite the controversial story to this day. Apprehend. Yes, it's from *apprehendere*. Literally, to seize."

I continued blinking at him.

"But it's not a spirit, you say?" Cornelius enquired.

"No. It was someone alive," I confirmed, although the question had never occurred to me. Of course it was someone alive.

"You're telling me that Patrice has been attacked?" Wiggles asked.

Cornelius chuckled. "He's a few beats behind. All of that George Michael has addled his brain."

"I'll have you know, there's no amount of George Michael that is too much!" Wiggles argued.

I took a breath and tried to get the conversation back under control.

"She's ok physically, I've checked her out. But she's shook up. I haven't let her talk about what happened because I know it's important you get the first report."

"That is important!" Wiggles said, as if the idea had only just occurred to him.

"She's in the den," I said, and pushed the door open. Wiggles walked in, followed by Cornelius, who grinned at the room as if he'd been hired to do a personal meet and greet. I shook my head and gave a discreet smile. Whoever that walrus of a man was, he was a character.

"'Patrice, are you happy to come and speak to me somewhere private?" Wiggles asked.

Patrice looked to Brandy, who gave her hand a squeeze, then nodded and rose from the seat.

"You can use the kitchen," I offered.

"Oh, they can, can they?! Sure, just use the kitchen! It's not used for anything else, is it! Barely a moment's work is done in that abandoned old space! I've got a good mind to hang up my apron springs, I'll have you..."

"Gilbert, dear. Maybe you could accompany them and make hot chocolates?" Mrs Claus suggested.

The irate elf beamed with pleasure once given a job. "Of course. Of course I can. I'll get to that right away."

The rest of us sat in an awkward silence. Sprout's foot tapped on the floor rhythmically and he glanced at his watch often. Brandy sat meek and mild, her body crouched in on itself to make herself as small as possible. Mrs Claus had picked up a ball of wool and was working on an intricately patterned jumper. August sat beside me picking at her fingernails, which was not something I'd seen her do before. I resisted the temptation to bat at her hand before she could make her cuticles look as battle-scarred as my own.

"So. Excited for Christmas?" Cornelius asked. He leaned forward in the seat he'd chosen as his own, his eyes large with excitement.

"Erm. Sure?" Sprout mumbled.

"Good, good. I've decided this is going to be a Christmas to remember. I'm planning on making my famous turkey dish."

"What's famous about it?" I asked, glad that Gilbert hadn't yet returned to the room or he would be mortally offended by me taking an interest in somebody else's food.

"Ah. Wouldn't you like to know?" Cornelius said with a laugh.

I smiled and waited, but he revealed nothing.

"Is it a secret recipe?" August asked.

"It's all about the butter. Not just butter butter. Although of course, better butter is better. The better the butter the better the turkey, that's no surprise. But my butter isn't just better butter. You follow?"

I nodded as if in a trance.

"I flavour my butter. By hand! Right in my kitchen in Tumble-down Manor. Flavoured butter transforms a meal. Transforms the turkey. Ah, you do a bit of kitchen work here, don't you?" Cornelius turned his attention to Gilbert as the elf returned to the room, and I braced myself.

"Excuse me?" Gilbert asked.

"You help out with the cooking and such?"

Gilbert crossed his arms across his spindly chest. "I'll have you know, I have a First Class Domestic Elf Degree and have risen through the ranks to run the management of Claus Cottage. As you might expect, that is the most admired position within Candy Cane

Hollow. I do not help out with the cooking. I am the cooking. I am the kitchen!"

We all stared at the tiny elf. He loved his dramatics, of course, but I'd never seen him appear so frustrated. His face was bright red and his whole body appeared to quiver in rage.

"You sure have a temper. I'll be sure to mention that to the police officer," Sprout called from across the room.

Gilbert turned on him, his anger deflating. "Whatever do you mean?"

Sprout shrugged. "There's a murderer on the loose. You weren't a fan of old Rudy, right?"

"Are you suggesting I'm some kind of common thug?" Gilbert asked. The idea of it would be laughable normally, but with tensions high, I found that my humour was less easy to find.

Sprout gave a lazy smile. "If the Santa hat fits..."

"Well! Well, this is new! I've never been so insulted in my life! First, I'm just the kitchen help, then I'm a murderer. What a sad day this is for Gilbert. Oh, I've got half a mind to..."

He was interrupted by the den door opening, and a dazed looking Patrice entered and flopped into the nearest chair.

Wiggles scanned the room and met my gaze, then opened his mouth to speak.

Gilbert approached him, arms out in front of him, hands together. "I guess you'll be wanting to cuff me now, officer?"

"I'll be what now?" Wiggles asked.

"It's okay. I know you have a duty to investigate. And I won't allow myself to cause a blemish on the Claus family's reputation. Take me in, officer! I'll come quietly!" Gilbert said with a flourish.

11

Wiggles furrowed his brows and looked closely at the elf who stood before him, awaiting an arrest that he clearly believed was imminent.

"You're confessing, are you?" Wiggles asked.

Gilbert gasped. "Of course I'm not! I'm guilty of nothing more than making the best hot chocolates this side of Mistletoe Moor!"

Wiggles chuckled. "Well, that's true enough. Holly, can I borrow you?"

"Is that really necessary, dear? Holly has a lot of work to do getting the Winter Ball ready," Mrs Claus asked as she paused, knitting needles frozen mid-stitch.

"I can assure you I won't get in the way of that. Nobody's looking forward to the Winter Ball more than I am," Wiggles confessed.

I rose from my chair and allowed him to lead me into the kitchen. Gilbert had managed to get back into the room before us, and was inspecting his beloved cupboards and crockery to make sure all was still in order.

"Would you give us just a moment?" Wiggles asked.

Gilbert gave a curt nod and retreated.

"How is she?" I asked.

"Patrice? Shook up, like you said. She's been through an awful lot. First she inherits millions, then her husband is killed, and then she's attacked."

I chewed the inside of my cheek for a moment as something troubled me. "That summary isn't quite accurate."

"What do you mean?"

"Patrice and Rudy. They were married, but estranged. He followed her here and she wasn't too pleased about it."

"Is that so?"

I nodded. "Why would she make out they were a couple to you?"

Wiggles shrugged his broad shoulders. "She had just suffered a bang to the head. She may not be thinking too straight."

I frowned. "Maybe she should go to the hospital for a more thorough check."

"Oh, no. She's with it. I tested that."

"You did?"

He nodded. "I quizzed her on some song lyrics, and let me tell you, that elf knows her George Michael."

"Oh. That's good. Do you have any idea who hurt her?"

Wiggles lowered his voice. "No clue at all. Cornelius got me thinking. Could it have been a spirit?"

"You can't believe that."

"He's smarter than he looks. And it was in a cemetery..."

"Surely if we go and check the cemetery, we'll be able to tell from the footprints in the snow whether Patrice was followed."

Wiggles clicked his fingers and then made a finger-gun, which he shot at me in an apparently congratulatory move. "That's a darn fine idea! I've got to get back to the stake out, though."

"What is this stake out about, anyway?" I asked.

Wiggles tapped the side of his nose. "I'm sworn to secrecy."

"Hmm. Well, maybe I could take August and we could check the cemetery."

"That's a great idea! Just as long as it doesn't interfere with your Winter Ball planning."

"Oh, no," I said, as I questioned the priorities of the police force in Candy Cane Hollow not for the first time.

"Well, that's sorted, then. Let me know if you need anything?"

"Sure," I croaked. "Oh. Wiggles? Do you have any leads for Rudy's death?"

Wiggles shot a glance at the den and then back to me. "It's somebody in this house. That's as much as I can tell you."

"It's - what?!"

Wiggles shrugged. "Something was slipped into his contact lens solution. That's why his eyes looked so darn scary. Ugh. They were like something out of a horror movie."

"And you think someone in Claus Cottage did that?"

"My money was on the housekeeper, but since Patrice was quiet about her marriage troubles, it's probably her."

"But she was attacked herself."

"So she says," Wiggles said with a lazy shrug. "No witnesses, no weapon, no serious damage. It's the perfect trick to get the heat away from her."

"Hmm. Hold on, did you say your money was on the housekeeper? You mean Gilbert?"

"Oh, yeah. He's buzzing with tension. It was only a matter of time before he snapped."

I considered this. Gilbert was buzzing with tension, and he snapped several times a day... usually when he imagined some slight against his cooking or general domestic ability.

But he would never hurt someone, would he?

"You've given me a lot to think about," I admitted.

Wiggles grinned. "That's good. Feel free to scout around a bit and look into things. It's not really something I can ask a junior officer to deal with, and I'm going to be wrapped up in this stake out for a while."

"I'll do what I can," I said.

Wiggles reached out and squeezed my arm. "That's the spirit. Have I told you my three best tips for solving a murder?"

"I don't think so," I said. It seemed like the kind of thing I would have remembered. Although it could be a challenge picking out the good information in between the Last Christmas playings.

"Well, here they are. Assume nothing. Test everything. Suspect everyone."

"Oh, wow. They're, erm..."

"Genius. I know," Wiggles said. He gave a cough and I turned to see Cornelius appear in the hallway behind us.

"Are we best to get back to it?" Cornelius asked.

"Yes. Yes we are. I was just sharing some tips with Holly."

"Ah. Good. I've got a tip for you, too," Cornelius said with a smile.

"Oh?"

"Don't wear stripes."

"Stripes?" I repeated.

He nodded, his jowls wobbling. "I know it seems unfair, and some people believe they are the exception to the rule. Or that one particular outfit is the exception. Trust me, it isn't. There's a reason that Americans make their prisoners wear stripes. It's the best deterrent there is."

I suspected that the overfilling of US prisons proved that point wasn't completely accurate, but who was I to argue?

"Well, I'll remember that," I said.

"You do that. Although, I admit, there's a photograph of yours truly wearing stripes. It was a fancy dress party. That's what I told Sly Stallone and it's what I'm telling you. So don't believe it if you hear otherwise, alright?"

"Yes, yes," I agreed hastily.

"Come on, Cornelius. The stake out awaits!" Wiggles said with a bang on the kitchen table.

12

I t was easier than I expected to convince August to take a nice stroll down to the cemetery with me, as long as she could call home first.

I could hear August's side of the conversation, followed by an occasional high pitched squeal of laughter.

"Who's a beautiful baby? Oh, yes you are! Oh, yes! You're mummy's Jeb-a-saurus! Raww!"

I smiled to myself. It really was so generous of August to come and visit me and leave her responsibilities at home.

When she was done with her call, we got back into our biggest, warmest clothes and braved the journey on foot rather than taking a sleigh.

"Thanks for coming with me," I said as we approached the cemetery's grand, wrought-iron gates.

"Are you kidding? The only thing I've investigated recently is The Search For The Missing Bib. We seem to lose a dozen a week."

"I can't believe my little sister is a mummy!" I exclaimed and squeezed her arm.

She grinned at me. "It is pretty wild, right? I don't feel grown up enough to have a baby. Never mind to be here trying to solve a murder! Where do we even start?"

"Well, right now we're looking for evidence. The snow can be great at preserving evidence. As long as there hasn't been a fresh snowfall, because that's really great at hiding evidence."

I saw the red and white police tape up ahead, cordoning off the area where Patrice had been attacked. A pinky tint to the snow confirmed that she had fallen and lost some blood, and the outline of her figure was still plain to see. I took out my phone and snapped a few photographs.

"Footprints!" August exclaimed. Neither of us entered the cordoned off area, but stood on the other side of the tape and gazed in. August had pointed out a set of footprints that were not much bigger than a reindeer's hooves.

"Elf footprints," I explained.

"Patrice's?"

The footprints ended where the outline of Patrice's fallen figure was.

"Looks like it," I said.

"And there are no other footprints around. What does that mean?" August asked.

I leaned in and examined the ground more closely. August was right. There were no other footprints in the area, which wasn't a surprise. This part of the cemetery featured graves that were old and in memory of people who were most likely no longer remembered. Not by anyone living, at least.

Why had Patrice been here?

Her explanation made sense, but was it the truth? Did she really come into the cemetery to try and think? She certainly had a lot to think about, between her inheritance and the death of her estranged husband.

A large branch lay on the ground, its jagged edges plain to see and obviously dangerous.

"Hmm," I murmured.

"What are you thinking?" August asked.

I pulled my phone out again and snapped some photographs of the branch.

"Murder weapon?"

"It could be," I said.

"But how did someone follow Patrice and attack her without leaving a track? And why leave the murder weapon behind?"

Cornelius' suggestion of a spirit attacker was one possibility, but I wrote it off straight off. There was no such thing as spirits.

I smiled at my baby sister. "You're good at this."

August rolled her eyes. "Do you think I should become a detective?"

"What? No! I think you're doing the most important job in the world being a mother."

"Really?" August asked.

"What's going on?" I asked her.

She looked down at the snow for a moment. "I always felt under so much pressure to grow up and be a professional, like you. Don't get me wrong, I'm so proud of you, Holly. And I know that being a doctor is a really important job. I just never wanted something like that... I want to keep a nice house and have a family and grow my own vegetables. It's silly, right?"

I scoffed. "Are you kidding me? I've always felt so envious of you! Your life is so put together and I'm just scrambling most of the time to remember what day it is."

"That's because you work crazy hours and have all of your patients to look after," August said.

I shrugged the compliment away. How could August feel envy, or admiration, for my life? She was the one with the family, with the house that was truly a home. She had the really important parts of life all figured out.

"I'm getting more of a balance here," I admitted.

"You are?"

I nodded. "My days are still full, but I'm actually surrounded by all of these people..."

"Like Mr Hunkalicious," August said in a sing-song voice.

I felt my cheeks flush and my stomach churned. "He's acting weird, sis."

"He is?"

"I've barely seen him lately. I know he's busy but we usually make time for each other. Now, I can hardly pin him down to say hello."

"Maybe he's just giving us time alone together?" August said.

I saw the hope in her face and switched back into strong big sister mode. I wouldn't let her worry about my problems.

"Sure. You're probably right. Anyway, I'm getting us distracted and we have a lot to do. We have the Ball to finish working on, and a murderer to catch!"

"Just another day in Candy Cane Hollow," August said with a grin as we returned our attention to the scene before us.

As we did, the skies opened and a fresh snowfall came down. I groaned, then snapped as many photographs as I could. The evidence would be lost under the snow within a matter of minutes judging by how quick the white was blanketing the ground.

On a whim, I dashed under the police tape and picked up the branch. August gasped.

"What are you doing?" She asked.

"Any evidence on this branch is going to be lost anyway. I can tell Wiggles to ignore my own DNA on it when the lab run their tests. It's either this or we lose a possible source of evidence," I explained.

"That all makes sense. We'll tell Wiggles that we made the decision together," August said, and held up her pinkie.

I grinned at her and linked my own little finger around hers. We hadn't made a pinkie promise in too many years.

Our pact was interrupted by a fat snowflake landing on the tip of August's nose. She crossed her eyes to examine it then shivered.

"Let's get out of this cold," I said, and we made a dash out of the cemetery and up the steep slope that would get us to Claus Cottage's elevated position.

I say we made a dash for it, but in reality we made a clumsy attempt to move through the heavily falling snow.

It was with a sigh of relief that I heard the tinkering sound of Last Christmas approaching.

The tiny Fiesta indicated and pulled over just in time as our visibility reduced dangerously close to zero.

"Hey, there! Didn't you hear there's a snowstorm on the way?" Wiggles called out of the driver's window. He had to yell to get his voice heard over George Michael's.

I laughed and gestured to the sky, which I could no longer see. "Isn't there always a snowstorm on the way?"

"Not like this. Jump in," Wiggles shouted, and it was only then that I noticed the man named Cornelius was in the small car beside him. The two of them looked comical in the tiny vehicle.

I did as I was told and opened the back door, then allowed August to climb in first.

"Glad we found you ladies. Maybe you can settle a dispute for us. Wiggles here is clearly a fan of a certain Christmas tune, but I've always enjoyed a bit of Mariah Carey's All I Want For Christmas. Which do you prefer?" Cornelius asked.

He and Wiggles both looked into the back seat expectantly, and I felt as much pressure as if they were a couple asking me to choose which of their children was my favourite.

"I like them both," I croaked weakly.

"Nonsense!" Cornelius' voice boomed inside the tiny car. He didn't seem to have to make any effort for his own voice to be heard over the music. "You must have a favourite!"

"I like Wizzard," August admitted with a grin.

"Wizzard?" Cornelius and Wiggles asked in unison.

August nodded. "I thought you'd prefer that one, Wiggles, since you live here in Candy Cane Hollow."

"Which one did they sing again?" Wiggles asked.

"I Wish It Could Be Christmas Every Day," August sang in tune. She'd always had a wonderful singing voice. If she ever relocated to Candy Cane Hollow, she'd be snapped up for the choir in no time.

"That's a good one! I like the fake snow in the music video too.

And all those adorable children! I wonder where they are nowadays and whether they still believe..." Cornelius mused.

"It's a perfectly good song," Wiggles admitted. "But you can't compare Roy Wood with George Michael!"

"Oh, I don't know. I just know that that song really makes me feel like Christmas has started."

"We used to watch it on illegal MTV," I reminded her.

August gasped. "Illegal MTV! I haven't thought about that for years!"

"Illegal MTV?" Wiggles asked with a particular interest in the word *illegal*. Trust me to admit to my life of crime in front of the chief of police!

"It was the funniest thing. Our dad was a bit of a wheeler dealer in his day. He managed to hook up this satellite dish and get MTV without paying for it. Sounds great, right?"

"Well, I..." Wiggles shifted in his seat.

"It was all well and good but he was tapping into German MTV somehow! Right here in England! We couldn't understand a word the presenters said and we only knew every third or fourth song!"

"And there was that Rammstein song out at the time. We were terrified of it, remember?" I prompted.

"Gosh, yes! The video of it showed these miners who discovered Snow White... they were all dirty and the song sounded so angry."

"We liked that one German band, though. The girl band. What were they called? No Angels? All Angels?"

August shrugged. "I don't remember them."

"No Angels. They were from the first series of Popstars. In fact, I ended up as their bodyguard for a short period of time," Cornelius said.

"You did what?" I asked in disbelief.

He shrugged his broad shoulders. "People see my impressive bulk and assume I'm in the security field. I usually refuse the work offers but that job sounded too interesting to decline. I believe young Sandy had quite the crush on me."

"Wow," I said, too stunned to attempt to string more of a sentence together.

I returned my attention to the road and saw that we were making incredibly slow progress. We'd have been quicker on foot, although we would have been soaked through.

"So, how bad is this snowstorm going to be?"

"Put it this way. The yetis are taking cover," Wiggles said.

"The yetis?" August asked with a tremble in her voice.

"They're friendly. Most of them, anyhow. They always know when a bad weather spell is coming. They feel it in their knees. Luckily, one of them owed me a favour and gave me a heads up. I pushed it out on the radio. Didn't you hear?"

I shook my head. "We've been busy. We needed to see you, actually. We went to the cemetery as you suggested, and there didn't seem to be footprints other than Patrice's. We did recover this log, though."

Wiggles nodded. "I did wonder why you were carrying a log around. Drop it in the boot and I'll get it sent for testing."

I turned in my seat and glanced at the cluttered detritus of the boot. "Do you have an evidence bag or something?"

Wiggles laughed. "Nothing big enough for that! It'll be fine in there, don't worry."

"I have a funny story about an evidence bag," Cornelius said, and I closed my eyes. I had a feeling the drive back to Claus Cottage was going to feel even longer than it was.

13

We finally reached Claus Cottage and made a dash across the courtyard to the safety and warmth of the inside. Wiggles and Cornelius refused our invitation to join us for a hot chocolate. They were keen to return to their stake out, and also planned on getting the log back to the station for testing.

We waved them off, then attempted to stomp off the majority of the snow from our boots, and pushed the front door open.

Gilbert stood in the hallway carrying a tray of hot chocolates. At the sight of us, his jaw dropped open and he shook his head.

"No, no, no! Don't traipse snow all across the house! I've just mopped these floors! Wait right there and do not move!" He commanded as he scurried into the den with the drinks.

August and I glanced at each other and raised our eyebrows.

Maybe it was my imagination but Gilbert did seem even more high-strung than his regular, Type A personality. Surely he couldn't have anything to do with Rudy's murder or the attack on Patrice?

"I've just had a thought," I whispered.

August leaned in.

"If another elf was careful enough, they could literally have followed Patrice across the cemetery in her own footprints."

"Another... elf?" August repeated, her eyes wide, as Gilbert returned from the den with an empty tray in his hands and a look of tortured frustration on his face.

"You've moved," Gilbert accused us.

"We haven't," I insisted.

"*You've* taken two steps forward, and *you've* taken at least a step and a half to the right. I don't know why I bother! I have a good mind to just hang up my..."

The den door opened and Mrs Claus poked her head out. Her mouth formed a comical 'o' shape as she took in the sight of August and me. No doubt we looked like drowned rats.

"Goodness gumdrops! You two look like drowned robins! Gilbert, fetch some hot towels."

"At once, Mrs Claus," Gilbert said and even gave a bow with a flourish as he dashed off towards the laundry room.

"The storm's started earlier than we expected. You poor dears. Get yourselves upstairs for hot showers and I'll have Gilbert make you some fresh soup," Mrs Claus suggested.

Neither August or I were going to argue with that idea.

We each selected a bathroom and showered, and as I enjoyed the hot water pummelling my frozen body, I considered Gilbert's behaviour. He was always stressed. I'd never seen the elf laidback, but over the last few days he seemed to be even closer to the edge than he usually was.

It was also clear that there was no love lost between him and Patrice, or Rudy.

But could I really see the elf as a murderer?

I mulled that question over as I dried myself and got changed. When I returned to the bedroom I was sharing with August, she was dressed in pink fluffy pyjamas, and I saw an identical outfit folded neatly on my bed.

"These are adorable!" I exclaimed.

August grinned. "Merry Christmas!"

"You bought these?"

She laughed. "I've been pulled into the tradition of matching

Christmas pyjamas for the family. Tom thinks it's silly but goes along with it, and of course Jeb won't be arguing about it for a few years yet. I thought it would be fun for us to have a set too."

"That's so thoughtful, thank you! Shall I put them on now?"

"That's up to you. I've been watching the news and it seems like we might be snowed in for a while."

I glanced at the small TV set up on top of the chest of drawers. A reporter stood outside Santa HQ, speaking into a microphone as the snow flurried furiously.

"We have some phone calls to make ready for the Winter Ball anyway. Now would probably be a good opportunity," I suggested.

August reached into her handbag and pulled out a notebook. The cover featured a photograph of her, Tom and Jeb, and was embossed in the corner with her initials.

"Personalised stationery?" I asked.

Her cheeks flushed. "It was a gift. Isn't it beautiful?"

I had to agree it was. In fact, if it was my notebook, I'd no doubt stash it away somewhere thinking it was too beautiful to use.

"I made a list of things we have left to do. We need to finalise numbers with the caterers, and you should probably run through your speech a few times."

"My speech? Very funny," I said with an eye roll as I pulled my clothes off and stepped into the pyjamas. They were so soft, it was like receiving a hug from the clothing.

"Don't joke with me," August said.

"I'm not falling for it. Nice try. These pyjamas are awesome," I said.

"I'm not joking. The organiser of the Winter Ball gives a speech. It's right here in the notes you sent me."

August reached back into her handbag and pulled out the information that Mrs Claus had provided me with. There were pages and pages of text, but Mrs Claus had told me not to worry too much about the details. She'd told me I had creative control over the event. She had never mentioned a speech.

August flicked through page after page, then cleared her throat and read aloud from the paper. "The organiser of the Winter Ball shall open the event with a small speech, to last no longer than thirty minutes. This speech should include gracious thanks to all involved in the event, a warm welcome to all in attendance, and at least two original and entertaining jokes."

"Original and entertaining jokes?! No longer than thirty minutes?!" I exclaimed. "Let me see that."

August held the paper out to me and my heart sank as I read the paragraph for myself.

She was not joking.

I had less than 24 hours to create a speech.

And find a murderer.

And get to the bottom of why Patrice had been left the entire estate of a complete stranger.

"I'm going to need your help," I said.

"That's what I'm here for," August said with a grin.

I pulled out my notepad and started jotting down ideas for the speech, while August watched and hummed a festive tune.

"Is that Last Christmas you're humming?" I asked.

"Oh! Sorry! It is pretty catchy, though. George Michael was so dreamy," August gushed.

"He sure was. I hear he also had great concentration that allowed him to stay focused on writing so many wonderful songs," I said. My hint was about as subtle as a shovel full of snow, but desperate times called for desperate measures.

August had the decency to allow her cheeks to flush apologetically. "Sorry. I was thinking, instead of a speech, how about a song?"

"You want me to write a song? Because that's so much easier than a speech?"

"It would be a speech... just to the tune of a Christmas song."

"Ha," I exclaimed.

"You want to put your own spin on the event, right? I'm guessing nobody else has ever turned their speech into a song?"

"Next you'll be suggesting I dance while singing it," I murmured.

"Goodness, no. I've seen you dance before. We don't need to inflict that on the poor people of Candy Cane Hollow. But you do have a lovely singing voice."

"Not as nice as yours," I said.

"Oh, hush. We both have the voices of angels."

"Hmm," I pondered. August's idea was unusual but perhaps it was genius. If I followed an existing song, that would give the speech a structure. I wouldn't be starting from nothing. Not really.

"It'll be fun!" August said with a grin.

I shrugged. "I don't have any better ideas. Let's work on this tonight. I want to speak to Patrice first."

14

We left our shared room and made our way downstairs, where the heat of the den welcomed us even before we pushed the heavy door open.

Mrs Claus glanced up at us from a chair by the fire, where she appeared to be knitting a scarf. Snowy was curled up by her feet, purring peacefully.

"Hello, dears. Feel better after those showers? I like the pyjamas."

I looked down and blushed. I'd completely forgotten we were dressed in the matching pyjamas that August had bought.

"Thank you so much for making me so welcome here, Mrs Claus. I love this place," August gushed as she walked across and plopped herself down in the chair across from Mrs Claus. She clearly had none of my reservations about our state of dress.

"Oh, it's our pleasure, August! It's marvellous to meet Holly's family. We do hope you'll return," Mrs Claus said. "If only there was a grand event planned. A wedding or something. That would be a fabulous chance to return with your own family!"

August grinned. "I do love a good wedding."

"Me too, dear!" Mrs Claus exclaimed. She placed her knitting down in her lap and leaned in close to my sister. I knew that the two of them spending time together would be trouble.

I cleared my throat. "Where is everyone?"

"Our guests are all in their rooms. Sprout and Brandy were quite emotional following the service, of course. And poor Patrice is so nervous of bumping into them that she's even requested taking her dinner into her room."

I gasped. "Will Gilbert allow such a thing?"

Mrs Claus pursed her rosy-red lips. "You know he won't. One of you will have to distract him and I'll take a plate upstairs."

"Mrs Claus, can I ask. Why did Artie not have a wake after the funeral?" August asked. She was clearly hanging on to her disappointment over missing a free buffet.

"Hmm. That's a good question, dear. I really don't know the answer. To be honest, I've been so focused on Rudy's death, I hadn't given it a thought."

I was pleased that she had turned the topic around to Rudy's death. It would allow me to ask her some questions without being too obvious. She was very concerned for my safety and wouldn't want to think that I was investigating.

"Did you hear anything unusual last night?" I asked.

She looked up at me. "I can't say that I did, but I do sleep awfully well. Especially at this time of year. The days are so full."

"Do you know that Wiggles believes someone in Claus Cottage is behind Rudy's death?" I asked.

Mrs Claus nodded. "I hope he's mistaken."

"But you don't know any of our guests well, do you?"

"That's true, but I do like to see the good in everyone. Patrice hardly seems like the kind of person who could hurt a snowman. Brandy is managing this stress awfully well in her condition. And Sprout... well, he's a tricky one, but it's a time of high emotion. I can't imagine how he must feel, knowing that he has lost any chance of reconciling with his father."

"He seems more worried about the money than the man," August said as she reached her hands out towards the fire and warmed them through.

"And then there's all of us to consider. If Wiggles is focusing his attention on Claus Cottage, we're all suspects. Not to mention Gilbert, Nick and Father Christmas."

Mrs Claus smiled. "Don't worry, Holly. Wiggles will get to the bottom of it all. We just need to sit back, wait out the storm, and trust our law enforcement."

"Doesn't it worry you that we're sharing a home with a murderer?" August asked, her eyes wide.

"Tsk. Not at all, dear. Whoever killed Rudy had their reasons and the long arm of the law will deal with them. I'm sure we're in no danger. If you'd feel safer, you could always find somewhere else to stay, but I'm sure that's not necessary."

"No, no, I want to stay here with you all. I guess we can lock our bedroom door tonight," August said with a smile. "I just need to get home safe."

"Of course you do. Your baby needs you," Mrs Claus said with a warm smile.

August grinned at the mention of Jeb. "It's so unlike me to be away from him. Tom has always been so busy with his work. He travels away and has these crazy deadlines. There are whole weeks that go by when Jeb and I barely see him."

"And you'll be reunited with him in no time," Mrs Claus reached out and squeezed my sister's hand.

The dinner bell rang out and we all filed into the dining room, where Gilbert had laid a place for everyone. To our surprise, Patrice was already at the table when we walked in. So much for staying in her bedroom.

"Are you okay, dear?"

Patrice nodded. "I realised how rude I was being, hiding out in that room. It must have appeared incredibly ungrateful after everything you've done. I've packed my things and I'll head home after we've eaten."

"Nonsense. Have you seen the storm?" A booming voice came from the doorway and we all turned to see Father Christmas in his trademark red outfit and big, black boots.

"I've told you before about not taking those off in the hallway, dear. Gilbert will have icicles if he sees you. Where are the slippers I bought for you?" Mrs Claus fussed.

Father Christmas obediently left the room and returned a few moments later, without his boots. Instead, he had on giant slippers with reindeer faces and antlers on.

"Much better, dear. Thank you," Mrs Claus said, and planted a kiss on her husband's bearded cheek.

Sprout and Brandy filed into the kitchen and took the remaining seats without saying a word to anyone. I decided not to draw any attention to their silence. Grief was a funny thing and could even make a person forget their manners.

"Where's Nick?" I asked.

Gilbert began to bring out the food and serve each person in turn. "He sends his apologies."

"He sends his apologies to you?" I asked, then heard the accusation in my voice. Nick could send his apologies to whomever he wanted. It sure was unusual though that he couldn't make dinner, and hadn't contacted me to say so.

"Yes, Holly, he sends his apologies to me. I am capable of taking a message, you know. It's not beyond me," Gilbert said as he placed slices of meat on each plate.

"Of course," I murmured. I would message Nick later and see what was going on. I was beginning to have the distinct feeling that he was avoiding me.

"How are you feeling now, Brandy, dear?" Mrs Claus asked.

Brandy blinked for a moment as if the question had brought her out of a trance. "I'm much better now, thank you, Mrs Claus."

"I'm glad to hear it. Brandy had a little fainting episode earlier this afternoon."

I looked at Brandy closer and saw that her face did look a little pale. Her hand rested on her stomach as it had before. Hold on. "Brandy, I'm the GP in town. Do you mind if I do a quick check on you?"

"Now?" Sprout asked, his face red.

"Please," I said, and rose from the table. Brandy did the same and followed me towards the doorway.

"Perfect! Absolutely perfect! I toil over a hot oven for hours, only to see my guests disappear one by one. I've got a good mind to..."

"Gilbert, dear. Is there any more of your delicious homemade cranberry sauce?"

"Yes! Yes, of course. I'll fetch it right this instant, Mrs Claus. I'm so glad you liked it. It's an old family recipe, passed down from generation to generation. There is a secret ingredient, but I can't tell you what it is."

"Is it cranberries, Gilly?" Father Christmas boomed.

"What? Wait... erm. No! Absolutely not!"

We closed the door behind us and I led Brandy into the dark den. I flicked on the lights and saw that the room was not empty after all. In the far corner, Nick paced the room, muttering to himself.

"Nick? I didn't realise you were here," I said.

He looked across at me but didn't smile. His dimple was not coming out to play, and its absence made my heart sink. There was something going on for sure.

But it would have to wait. I had a suspicion about Brandy and my oath as a doctor meant that she was my priority at that moment.

"I need to speak to Brandy alone for a moment. Do you mind?" I asked.

He gave a quick nod of his head and scarpered out of the room without a goodbye.

"He's up to something," Brandy said as the door closed behind him.

I gave a nervous laugh. "Time of the year, I'm sure. Everyone goes a little frantic as Christmas approaches."

"So, you want to check on me? It's not necessary, really."

"Brandy, is there anything I should know about your physical health. Your condition, as it were?" I asked.

Brandy couldn't keep the emotions from her face. She grinned, then her eyes filled, and then she began to sob.

"You're pregnant, aren't you?"

15

S he nodded and attempted to get her breath, to allow her to
speak to me.

"It's okay. I know it's a huge thing. Did it come as a
surprise?"

She sucked in a huge gasp of air and nodded again.

"You must be feeling all kinds of emotions. That's natural. And
the fainting is probably natural too. Those early pregnancy days can
be really tough physically. It is important that you get checked out,
though. Have you seen your doctor yet?"

Her white curls bounced as she shook her head.

"Okay, well that's a priority when you get home. There are supple-
ments you'll need to start taking and appointments that the doctor
will get scheduled for you. Right now, let me check some things for
you."

Brandy was compliant and deep in thought as I checked her
blood pressure, temperature and heart rate. She had stopped crying
but her breath was irregular and ragged.

"Do you want to lie back and I'll see if I can listen to baby?" I
asked.

She nodded and pressed the button that allowed the chair to

transform into a recliner. I pulled up her top and saw the swelling of her stomach. Her baggy clothes hid it well. She was further along than I'd expected.

I pushed and poked, checking that everything felt healthy, then placed my stethoscope on her stomach. A regular, strong heartbeat. Always a blessing and a relief to hear.

"If I had to guess, I'd say you're almost six months pregnant. Baby has a good, strong heartbeat. Here, do you want to listen?" I asked.

She nodded and I transferred the ear pieces to her while I held the other end in place on her stomach. I knew the moment she had heard her baby as she began to cry again and covered her mouth.

I smiled. It was an incredible moment.

"Do you want me to get Sprout in here?" I asked.

Her expression changed and she shook her head, pulled the ear pieces out and made to move back to a sitting position.

"Does he know?" I asked gently.

She nodded.

"Is he happy about it?"

She scoffed and rolled her eyes. "Of course he is. He thinks we'll be this perfect little family. He doesn't realise how out of touch he is."

"I know there's a lot to think about, but if you both want this baby, I'm sure you can make the details work," I said. I was used to women often having more complicated feelings about a pregnancy than their spouse, which wasn't a surprise.

"You don't understand. We can't afford a baby! We have no money!"

"Really?" I asked, as I remembered the fur coat that Sprout had arrived at Claus Cottage wearing. He had certainly seemed like a man of financial means to me. But appearances could be deceiving.

"Sprout's always got some business idea he's working on, but none of them stick. He just doesn't have his father's head for business."

"Maybe he'll get a steady job now he knows about the responsibilities on the way," I suggested as I packed my stethoscope away.

"He'd rather die than work a steady job. He's a Rumples! They're very entrepreneurial. I've put up with a lot over the years. There have been months where we've eaten nothing but Festive Feast for breakfast, lunch and dinner."

"Really? You guys ate that even after the fall out?"

"Sprout still had a family discount. He didn't like eating it, trust me, but there wasn't money for anything else. I didn't mind it because I believed he'd make it all work out one day, but it's just been failure after failure. You know he actually watched Frozen and decided to try being an ice seller? Who could have taken that business idea from that film?!"

"Hmm. Yeah, I've only seen it once but I seem to remember the joke being that selling ice in the frozen tundra had a bit of a supply and demand problem," I agreed.

"Exactly!"

I kneeled down so I was at eye level with Brandy. "Listen to me. I can understand how scary everything must feel right now. But all of those practical issues can be sorted out. Trust me."

She snivelled and looked deep into my eyes. "Do you have children?"

My cheeks flushed. "Oh, no. No, I don't. But I've cared for a lot of people over the years who had worries just like yours. It always turns out okay."

She shook her head and began to cry again, but before I could ask her what was wrong, the den door was pushed open and Sprout appeared in the doorway, his face red and stern.

"What's going on? What have you done to her?" He asked me, as he stormed across the room and placed himself right in between me and his wife.

"I was just checking she was okay after her fainting earlier," I explained.

"And?"

"And she is," I said with a smile.

"Then it sounds to me like your work here is done," Sprout said, his arms crossed.

I frowned. If I was at work, and this was happening in a patient's appointment, I'd ask the man to leave and go through some routine domestic violence checks with the woman. But Brandy wasn't my patient, and Sprout had buried his father earlier that day.

"I'm here if you need me. Either of you," I said, and I left them alone in the den and returned to the kitchen.

**

"Bingo?" Gilbert asked as I returned to my seat at the table. He had again joined us for the meal, although his plate of food was untouched.

"I haven't been there in years," Patrice said with a shake of her head.

"What's happening?" I whispered.

"Gilbert's trying to jog Patrice's memory of where she could have met Artie," August answered.

I nodded. It was as good an idea as any. I listened as I began to eat dinner. I hadn't realised just how hungry I was.

"Candy Cane Custody?"

"What? I've never been to jail!" Patrice exclaimed.

"Not even to bail out that no good husband?" Gilbert asked.

"Gilbert!" Mrs Claus exclaimed.

"Sorry. That no good husband, Santa rest his soul," Gilbert quipped.

Mrs Claus shook her head as if he was beyond her help.

"Marching band?"

"Nope."

"Sleigh Bells Solicitors?"

"No... wait..." Patrice froze in place, as if the thought might make a run for it if she so much as moved. Her knife and fork remained in her hands, midway through cutting a slice of meat.

"That rings a bell, dear?" Mrs Claus asked.

"Rings a sleigh bell!" Gilbert quipped, then descended into maniacal laughter at his own joke.

"Perhaps. I did see them. They drew up the divorce papers for me," Patrice said.

"The papers that Rudy refused to sign," Gilbert added, helpfully.

"Does anything stand out in your memory from the appointment?" I asked.

""Everything!" Patrice winced. "It was awful. I was in such a state that day. I went along to the appointment and I think part of me was hoping the lawyer would recommend I gave it another chance."

"I'm guessing they didn't?"

Patrice shook her head. "The lawyer was very nice, but she told me some things I didn't want to hear. She said that Rudy had been controlling me for years. I got overwhelmed and I asked for some peace and... oh... oh my... Heavens above..."

"What is it, dear? What have you remembered?"

"It was him!"

"Artie?"

Patrice nodded furiously. "He was in the reception area and I burst through in tears."

"You spoke to him?"

"No. No, we didn't speak. He went into his pocket and gave me a tissue. That's all he did. But I got my phone out and rang my mother, and I told her everything. She'd never been a fan of Rudy. She told me to get back in the room and get the papers sorted. I told her I was scared of living alone, scared of surviving on my own."

"Did you say you were worried about money, dear?"

"I don't think so. Rudy never contributed much to the house. What little he did earn, he spent... and plenty more besides that. Things will always be tight on my wages, but I'm actually a little better off without him."

"But if Artie heard your conversation with your mum, he could have got the impression you were worried about money?" I asked.

"Yes, I guess so. He would have known I was a woman about to ask for a divorce and try going it alone."

August and I glanced at each other. "We need to see Artie's solicitor."

16

The snow had cleared enough for us to get to the home of Bertram Smythe, who had been Artie's solicitor.

The old man answered the door and peered at us through thick, heavyset spectacles.

"Good evening ladies. Can I help you?" I was struck again by his voice. It was deep and refined and spoke of a long career filled with many successes and even more bottles of whisky from grateful clients.

"We'd like to speak to you about Artie Rumples. Can we come in?"

"Of course," he said. He opened the grand front door fully and we stood in a large hallway with him, until we realised we would go no further until we took off our snow boots.

"My apologies. Gloria hates when snow is spread through the house," he said with a smile that suggested he wasn't sorry at all. He was the great lawyer after all.

Once we were adequately clean, Bertram asked us to follow him into what was a deeply impressive home study. Filled with a mahogany desk and bookcases that must have been custom built to fill the space, and warmed by an open fire, it was the kind of space I would have loved to have available to me.

"This place is amazing," I complimented.

"Please, take a seat," he said as he lowered himself carefully into his wingback chair. August and I sat across from him. August clasped her hands across her lap while I held a notepad and pen in my own.

"Thank you for letting us in," I said.

"I trust you'll be okay without drinks? The help has finished for the evening and I do hate to call her back upstairs," Bertram said. Clearly the idea of him making us drinks himself was not an option.

"Of course. We'll be quick. We've been assisting the beneficiary of Artie's estate. She hasn't been able to work out why Artie selected her. I don't suppose you can share anything with us?"

"Absolutely not. The tiny issue of a person's death doesn't affect my client confidentiality. You should know that as a doctor."

"They're actually different levels of confidentiality," I shot back before realising how tetchy my voice might come across.

"Yes, of course. Only a lawyer client privilege is unbreakable," Bertram said as he uncorked a bottle of scotch and poured himself a generous glug in an already wet glass.

"The beneficiary has remembered a chance encounter with Artie at your offices, on the day she began divorce proceedings. We believe that encounter gave Artie the idea of changing his will."

Bertram laughed. "Artie changed his will frequently. There were at least two periods in the last few years when I was the sole beneficiary. You can imagine how pleased I was when he came in and announced he wanted to make changes then!"

"And what prompted all of those changes?"

Bertram shrugged. His concerns about confidentiality had disappeared out of the window as soon as the whisky had been opened.

"I couldn't say. I don't believe Artie could say. He was a man with a great fortune and no natural way of passing it along."

"He wouldn't have wanted Sprout to inherit?"

A dark cloud passed over Bertram's face. "After what that boy did? No chance at all. He broke his poor father's heart. There are many,

many things I can't tell you about Artie, but I can tell you very clearly that he did not want his son to inherit a penny. Not while they remained estranged. A single phone call from Sprout would have changed everything, but the boy is too stubborn by far. And I told him as much when I saw him with his wife at Claus Cottage and he demanded that I put things right!"

"You were this direct with him?" I asked.

"Even more so! I called Artie a friend, not just a client. I saw the pain that the boy caused him. Artie allowed him to keep all of the benefits that came from being his son. The discounts, the car, the health insurance. Artie sent him letters, they all came back unopened. No, it was not good what he did to the man. Not good at all."

"I'll be happy to feed that back to Patrice. It will help make her decision a little easier. It's been very confusing for her."

Bertram grinned. "I've spent Artie's fortune a hundred times over, in my head. Oh, the fun she will have!"

"I think she'll use it to do some good, actually," I said.

Bertram raised his eyebrows and blinked at me. "Well, that too, of course. Good for her. Now, allow me to show you out."

And show us out, he did. Our winter boots were barely back on our feet before he pushed the heavy door closed behind us and returned to his whisky.

"He was a character," August said. "But he seems to have looked out for Artie's best interests. I hope Patrice will keep the money."

"Me too. I have a feeling that it's ended up with the best person," I agreed.

We stomped back through the snow to our sleigh, and August doused Betty in another spritz of her perfume.

"You'll have to put this on your Christmas list," August instructed the reindeer. I rolled my eyes. Reindeer didn't get Christmas presents.

"Or you'll have to come back with another bottle," I suggested.

August grinned. The tinny sound of her phone ringing disturbed us, and she answered right away.

"Tom? What's wrong? We don't have a call scheduled for this time. Is Jeb okay? Has something happened?"

I smiled to myself. Only my sister could schedule call times to speak to her husband.

"That's awful. Can they do that?" She said, and the smile disappeared from my face as I realised that she was receiving bad news. Something had happened.

"You need to speak to HR and get some advice. And check your contract, it's in the turqoise filing cabinet, second drawer down. Do you need me to come home?"

My heart sank for a moment as I remembered that Candy Cane Hollow was merely borrowing my sister from her real life. She would return home... hopefully tomorrow, but maybe sooner if needed. She had a family who needed her. Not to mention whatever new situation had arisen.

"Well, yeah. I mean, I guess. Okay, okay. Call me later. Love you," August ended the call and stared straight ahead, processing whatever Tom had just told her.

"Is everything okay?"

"I've got no idea. Tom's just been fired."

"He's... what?"

"He left early today to fetch Jeb from nursery and his boss has basically told him not to show his face again," August said as she buried her head in her hands.

"What? That's not allowed, surely?"

"I don't know. He wasn't strictly employed by them, he was freelance... so I guess they can do what they want? HR won't even speak to him because he's not on their payroll as an employee."

"August, that's awful. Look, I have some savings, you can have as much as you need to tide you all over. I won't see you struggle," I said.

"Thanks. That's kind. This is just the worst time to get news like this. Right before Christmas! The job market is so up and down, apparently. Tom's been ringing all of his contacts and there are no jobs around."

I felt heat flush my cheeks as I realised the question I needed to ask next. I should have already known the answer. "What exactly does Tom do?"

August groaned. "Ugh. He's in some kind of, like, strategic organisation? Systems implementation?"

I stared at her blankly. "I'm sorry. What does that mean in every day English?"

August shrugged. "I try not to ask. Basically, I think he oversees really big projects. Like, really, really big projects."

I nodded to show my understanding, as the beginning of an idea began to fizz away in my mind.

"Does he want you to go home early?" I asked.

"No. There's nothing I can do by being there. He told me to just try and relax."

"Would it help if I distracted you?" I asked.

"Always," August said with a laugh. I filled her in on my conversation with Brandy, and Sprout's weird behaviour when he saw me with her.

"Sprout seems like a serious jerk," August said.

"You should work on being less subtle. If you've got an opinion, just say it," I teased.

"I'm serious. He's made his pregnant wife feel rotten. He's rude to everyone. And he caused his father so much pain! Not to mention that he didn't even organise a wake!"

"You're really hanging on to the lack of a wake, sis," I said with a smile as we pulled up at Claus Cottage.

Patrice stood on the doorstep and tried to duck into the shadows as she saw us.

"Hey! Everything okay?" I called out to her from the sleigh.

She reluctantly accepted that she had been seen and padded across the blanketed snow. "I'm heading home. Thanks for everything."

"Don't you want to stay a while longer?" I asked.

"You shouldn't be leaving in the dark. We still don't know who attacked you."

"Actually, we do," I said with a smile.

"You do? Well, I guess I could come in for a little longer. I just don't want to outstay my welcome. Not to mention the fact that Sprout looks furious every time he lays eyes on me."

"Don't you worry about him," I said.

The three of us walked around the side of Claus Cottage together, to the stables where the reindeer bedded down for the night. Even August pitched in unfastening the animals' harnesses and showing each reindeer to their stable.

"You let me know if you get bored of that jobless bum," Matix whinnied as August lead him across the stable courtyard.

August laughed. "I'll bear you in mind if I'm looking for a more... hairy... companion."

"Don't think about it too much. A reindeer like me won't be on the market for long," Matix said.

I grinned and shook my head.

I had hoped my sister would feel at home in Candy Cane Hollow, but I could never have predicted that one of the reindeer would develop a crush on her.

"Do you really know who attacked me?" Patrice asked me when we had got all of the reindeer back in their stables for the night, each of them with an extra carrot to thank them for their hard work in the snow.

"I do. And not just that, I know what happened to Rudy," I said.

"Seriously?" Patrice asked. Her face was the image of complex, and conflicting, emotions. "I know now that it was the right thing to do, to separate with him. But I never would have wanted him to be hurt or suffer. If you can get his killer caught, I'll be eternally grateful."

"I know," I said. Their marriage hadn't worked, but that didn't mean they had to hate each other. It was clear to me that Patrice wanted to move on with her life while Rudy moved on with his.

We returned to the front of Claus Cottage just as Wiggles pulled up. The tune of Last Christmas was ominously missing.

17

"Don't worry. There's some kind of electric fault. Everything in the darn car works apart from the CD player! Would you believe it?" Wiggles asked as he walked past us into the house.

I watched as Cornelius staggered to his feet from out of the passenger side of the car. He glanced across at Wiggles, who was walking away from us, and then waved a CD in the air.

"I couldn't take it one more time! I'll have that tune in my head until the day I die, I swear. I've hidden it and convinced him that the system's malfunctioning," Cornelius confided with a grin.

I laughed and we all made our way into the house.

"What can I do for you?" I asked Wiggles as we all stamped our feet in the hallway.

"I have the lab results back on the log," he said.

"That was quick," I said with surprise.

"They owed me a favour," he shrugged.

"Let me guess. No DNA evidence apart from my own? And Patrice's, of course."

"Bingo. I know it's disappointing, but the snow wreaks havoc with evidence out here," Wiggles explained.

"No, it makes sense. The reason there's no DNA is because there was no attacker."

"What?" August asked.

"Huh?" Wiggles asked.

"I can promise you there was. Someone took me out with a real blow to the head," Patrice explained.

Only Cornelius gave me a grin of recognition that showed he was on the same page as me.

"Patrice, you were walking in a cemetery during a snowstorm. We've had crazy snow, even for Candy Cane Hollow. That branch simply snapped and gave way under the weight of the snow. It was the branch that hit you, not a person," I explained.

Patrice opened her mouth but said nothing.

"Is that my cousin Patrice speechless? Well, Santa help us, what's next?" Gilbert said as he breezed out from the kitchen with a tray of hot chocolates. We all grabbed one and downed it and he nodded approvingly.

"It was just an accident," Patrice said as the truth sank in. "I'm not in danger?"

"No, you're not in danger. Now let's get into the den and solve this case, once and for all," I said.

**

The scene in the den was stiflingly quiet.

Mrs Claus had picked up her knitting again, and Brandy and Sprout sat next to each other, saying nothing. Father Christmas and Nick were nowhere in sight.

"They've been called to Santa HQ, dear," Mrs Claus explained as she saw me glancing around the room.

Snowy came up to August purring, then draped herself around my sister's legs.

"Let's all take a seat. I'm going to share what happened to Rudy," I said.

"You are? You're not police," Brandy objected.

"She's a consultant," Wiggles said with a nod to me, to get started.

"We were unsure at first whether Rudy's death was natural or not.

The only sign of injury he had was this awful redness to the whole of his eyes. Highly unusual. Not something I'd ever seen before, and I told Wiggles it reminded me of an allergic reaction."

"Did he have allergies, dear?" Mrs Claus asked Patrice, who grimaced and shook her head to indicate that she was unsure.

"That's the thing with allergies. An allergic substance is just anything we react badly to. You may react badly to peanuts, but the next person doesn't. There are things that we all react badly to, though, and we don't class those as allergies. We simply say those things are harmful to us. Toxic. Poisonous. Deadly."

"Is this relevant?" Sprout asked. "Not to mention, why are we here for this? Rudy seemed like a horrid man but I didn't kill him. Shall we show ourselves out?"

"You'll stay where you are," Wiggles said in a surprisingly authoritative voice.

Sprout shifted in his seat to show that he disliked the order, but he didn't try to move.

"It is relevant, because we know that Rudy was killed by a toxic substance that was placed into the contact lens solution he carried. He took his contacts out when he went to bed and placed them in the solution until the next day."

"And somebody added something to that solution? That's awful," Patrice breathed.

I nodded. "It is. By the time Rudy would have realised that something was wrong, it was too late."

"So, who did it?" Sprout asked.

"Well, we have to ask who would have wanted Rudy dead. And sadly there are a few people with motives. Patrice had been trying to get away from him for months. He wouldn't give up on their marriage, and even trailed her here. Maybe killing him was the only way to get rid of him?"

"Makes sense. She's also the person most likely to have known he had contact lens solution with him," Sprout said.

"Yes. Although in my experience, things don't line up that neatly."

"I have an alibi," Patrice murmured.

"Oh! Of course she remembers it now! Go on, spill the details," Sprout said with a laugh.

"I didn't spend the night alone," she said, and her cheeks flushed.

Sprout jumped from his chair. "She did it! Don't you see? She's a charlatan! She conned my father and now she's got her teeth into her next con!"

"That's not true!" Patrice objected.

"We'll need to speak to the person you spent the night with," Wiggles said, his voice low and respectful.

Patrice nodded.

"It was me," Gilbert's reedy voice came from the doorway.

I turned and stared at him, my mouth open. "You, Gilbert?"

"I wondered why you came downstairs, dear, when that dreadful scream woke us all," Mrs Claus said. "You've always been so insistent that you sleep next to the kitchen."

Gilbert had turned a scorching shade of red, right to the tips of his pointed ears. "What can I say? I can't resist her jokes and aimless chatter. I'm like a sugar addict in a candy cane field when I'm around her."

"There's no crime in that," Wiggles said, although he didn't sound too sure.

"Of course he's going to side with one of his own kind!" Sprout shouted.

"Let's look at other people. Why else could someone want Rudy out of the way? Well, the obvious thing is that he was so vocal about Patrice keeping the inheritance. She was really wavering for a while, and it was Rudy who was determined that she should keep the money. With him out of the way, it would be easier to persuade Patrice to hand the inheritance over, right?"

Sprout shrugged his meaty shoulders. "Doubtful. Who in their right mind would just give up a life-changing sum of money like that?"

"Lots of people, if they believed it was the right thing to do. Take your father's solicitor, for example. He told me that Artie changed his Will frequently. It seemed that the poor old man was at a loss of knowing what to do with his wealth. He should have had a son to pass it on to, but that son had made it clear he wanted nothing to do with him."

"What's that got to do with old Bertie?"

"Your father made him the beneficiary. Twice. If nobody would ever part with that kind of money, the solicitor would have found a way to persuade your dad not to make any further changes. But he didn't. He drafted the new Wills himself, time and time again, knowing that he was in effect costing himself millions of pounds."

"That's not the same," Brandy said.

"It's similar enough. Patrice is reasonable. She was conflicted. With the right time and encouragement, she could have been convinced to hand the money over."

"Especially if she knew about the pregnancy," Sprout agreed.

"The pregnancy? You're pregnant, Brandy?" Patrice said with a gasp.

She nodded and her eyes filled with tears.

"Oh, goodness. Of course I would have wanted you to have the money if I'd known," Patrice said as she made a dash towards Brandy's side.

"Just hold on," I warned. "Rudy was the one getting in the way of Sprout claiming his inheritance. Everything would slot into place if he was out of the equation, right Sprout?"

"I guess so," Sprout agreed.

"So you killed him?" August asked the man.

"What? No! I was fast asleep. I sleep like the dead. Every night, without fail," Sprout boasted.

"I did hear snoring," August admitted.

"That'll be me," Sprout said with a grin.

"You don't sleep so easily lately, right, Brandy?"

She gave me a weak smile. "It's the pregnancy."

"Oh, tell me about it. When I was pregnant I barely got five hours a night. And then you have a baby at the end of the process who makes even five hours feel like a luxury," August exclaimed.

"You got up? You were wandering the house?" I asked.

Brandy looked down into her lap. "I just couldn't sleep. I'm so worried about money."

"I've told you I'll sort it all out," Sprout snapped at her.

"Let her speak," August told him. She was feisty when she wanted to be.

"I know you keep saying that, but I don't see any money coming in. I couldn't stop thinking about how I'll pay for nappies and clothes and everything else a baby needs. This should be the happiest time of my life and I'm worried sick, and you just won't listen to me!"

Sprout rolled his eyes.

"What happened?" I pushed.

"I was just down here drinking a hot chocolate..."

Gilbert gasped. "You made it yourself?"

Brandy nodded. "My thoughts ran away with me. Maybe it was the tiredness. I was so tired. I hated how Rudy had spoken to you, Patrice. I didn't like that he'd followed you out here. I thought that somebody needed to teach him a lesson, and I remembered that he'd come down in those ridiculous glasses, so I knew he'd have contact solution in the bathroom."

"Brandy, we can get a lawyer. Don't say any more," Sprout encouraged.

"Mr Rumples is right. You're entitled to a lawyer if you want one," Wiggles agreed.

"No, no. I'm done with pretending."

"Pretending?" Sprout scoffed.

"Yes! Everything is fake! You're wearing that fur coat you love but our rent hasn't been paid for three months! I'm done with it all. I added the bleach to the contact lens solution. It was me. I did it. You can take me in now," Brandy said.

"You killed him?" Patrice asked with a gasp. Her hand shot to her mouth and her eyes grew wide.

Brandy shook her head and began to cry. "I had no idea he'd die. I just wanted to do something to get back at him for how awful he had been. I swear on Santa's life that I never thought for a second it could be lethal. I've been adding that stuff to Sprout's coffee for months when he particularly annoys me. It's my little rage against the hormones, I guess."

"You've been what?" Sprout asked, his face pinched with anger.

"Let's all calm down," Cornelius suggested. "This all reminds me of a time I mixed up the salt and the sugar. I made my sister quite the bitter cup of tea. And she wasn't one for laughing things off. Not at that point of her life, anyway."

"That's hardly the same! You've been poisoning me, woman?" Sprout roared from his chair.

Brandy cowered in her seat and I watched with pride as August placed herself in between the two of them.

"You need to sit down, calm down and talk to her with some respect," August commanded. She made a terrifying figure, with her legs wide apart, her arms crossed and her lips pursed. She always had been the toughest of the two of us.

"It didn't do any harm. You never even noticed," Brandy said with a shrug.

"You've killed a man! That could have been me! I'll sue you, Brandy, for everything you've got!"

Brandy scoffed. "I've got nothing. You and your shopping habits have made sure of that."

"If we could stay focused on Rudy, perhaps?" I interrupted.

Everyone stopped the argument they were involved in and looked at me expectantly.

"Brandy, he's dead because of you, whether you meant to hurt him or not. That's manslaughter, right?" I looked at Wiggles.

The officer looked at Brandy, then Patrice, and shrugged his broad shoulders. "There are defences. Mitigating circumstances. There's the question of whether someone is fit to be held criminally responsible. Those are all talks to have with a lawyer, of course."

"Of course," I said. There was hope for her. That would have to be enough right now.

"In the meantime, Brandy Rumples, I'm arresting you on suspicion of manslaughter. Please follow me and we'll get you nice and comfortable in Candy Cane Custody. I make a mean hot chocolate, you know. The best in Candy Cane Hollow, some people say!"

"They do not," Gilbert hissed under his breath.

Brandy stood from her seat and looked not at her husband, but at Patrice. "I really am sorry."

"It's okay. I believe that it was an accident. And, erm, if you need bail money, give me a call?"

18

August and I had been sniping at each other most of the afternoon as we worked on the finishing touches for the Winter Ball. It was all fine. We were sisters, and we both liked things to be right. It was a blessing to have been in her company long enough to have started to annoy each other... that hadn't happened in years.

Finally, everything was ready and we were able to return to Claus Cottage to dress in our evening gowns. The kitchen staff were already working on the feast, and Michael Bauble had arrived with his entourage to prepare in the dressing room. His demands included an old rotary telephone, twelve cases of sparkling water, and a disco ball.

I hadn't dared to enquire about what kind of warm up technique he was using that required all of those things. He put on a good show and that was all that mattered.

We had taken a small sleigh to the Festival Hall, pulled by Betty and Einstein. When we jumped in and asked them to take us home, Betty became emotional.

"I can't believe that you, and that wonderful perfume, are leaving us," she sniffled. I tried not to be insulted by the show of emotion, which far exceeded anything I'd ever received from her.

"I'm sure I'll be back in no time," August reassured her, and away we sped through the snowy streets.

The excitement in the air was even more palpable than normal. Christmas was another day closer, and the whole of Candy Cane Hollow was looking forward to the Winter Ball. It was no secret that it was my first solo event, and I felt the weight of the town's expectations on me. It was going to be a big night.

"That's strange," I said as we parked outside Claus Cottage. Wiggles' car was parked outside and my heart sank. Surely there hadn't been another crime?

"Is everything okay?" I asked as we pushed open the front door and found the police officer in the hallway, bopping back and forth on the heels of his feet while humming the tune of his favourite song.

"All good!" Wiggles said with a grin.

"How is Brandy doing?" I asked.

Wiggles gave a chuckle. "She's doing alright. She's going to plead guilty. And in the meantime, I've given her the softest pillows we have available."

I smiled to myself. "She's probably living in more luxury than she did at home."

"I should sure hope so. People can make mistakes, but they still deserve the finest bedding."

"I guess they do," I said. "Do you think Sprout will make an appearance tonight?"

"Last I heard he was making a hasty exit before the bailiffs turn up and take his furniture in lieu of payment. I have seen Patrice, though. She was the first one in the station this morning with freshly baked cookies for Brandy."

"They seem to have made a real friendship," I mused.

Wiggles nodded his agreement. "And long may it last."

There was an awkward silence for a few moments. "I'm sorry, I don't mean to sound rude, but are you here for a reason or a social call?"

"Oh! I forgot. I found a couple of waifs and strays wandering the street, and I figured where better to take them to than Claus Cottage!"

Right at that moment, there came a squeal of excitement from the den and August gasped.

"Jeb?" She shouted, and pushed open the door to the den. We quickly followed and watched with happiness as she grabbed her baby son from the plush carpet and smothered him in kisses.

"Hello, Tom," I greeted her husband, who sat by the fire warming himself.

"So, I'm either very drunk or overtired, because I swear I was just made a hot chocolate by an elf," he said as he rose from the chair and planted a kiss on my cheek.

"Ah. Yes. We'll explain everything. What are you two doing here?"

"It's the strangest thing. I just had this sense that we needed to get in the car and drive. I can't even remember most of the journey. We just arrived here and then I think it was a policeman? He picked us up and it was... well... that guy really loves George Michael."

I laughed and pulled my brother-in-law in for a hug. "It's so good to see you! You can stay for the Winter Ball tonight, right?"

"I guess?" Tom said.

"Yay! And oh my goodness, look at you, Mr Jeb! How quick are you growing?" I cooed over my baby nephew, who clung to August with a fierce and possessive love. "Oh, you're angry I stole your mamma away, are you? Well, buddy, we have to share her. I loved her first. Oh yes I did. Oh yes I did!"

I looked up to see Mrs Claus watching me and wiping a tear from her eye. "You'll make a marvellous mother one day, Holly."

I groaned as I realised just how far into the future her hopes were going. I still hadn't had a chance to pin Nick down for a talk, and the longer we carried on in this strange silence, the more I knew that any talk we did have would only end badly.

It was time to face the facts.

Whatever Nick and I had, he was over it.

He was over me.

I was about to be dumped by Santa.

I could imagine the whole of my future dating life as I tried to get other men to measure up against Nick. It was an impossible task.

"You two really need to get ready. We have to leave in a few moments," Mrs Claus said.

August and I glanced at our watches, gasped, handed Jeb over to Tom, and took the stairs two at a time. We helped each other into our matching gowns - mine was a festive deep shade of red and August's was a cool gold.

I fixed my hair up while she allowed hers to tumble freely around her face.

"If I tie it up, Jeb will only pull it out again," she said with a laugh. Being reunited with her son had given her an extra bounce and I loved to see it.

"You look exquisite," I said.

"And you, my darling big sister, look marvellous. Let's show these people how to party!"
**

We were greeted at the Festival Hall by elves who poured us each a welcome drink of bubbly champagne. There was something about champagne that made me feel like a child pretending to be a grown up, and I felt the nervous giggles building in me.

We were a few minutes late, mainly because Betty had insisted on one last spray of Chanel before she felt able to pull the sleigh, and the perfume set Einstein off with a sneezing fit.

For that reason, we were among the last to arrive. People in Candy Cane Hollow liked to arrive everywhere prompt.

I waved at familiar faces as we weaved our way through the bar to the top table that was reserved for us. Ginger Rumples dashed across to me, looking heavenly in an emerald green dress, and pulled me into a bear hug.

"Hey, you!" She squealed. There was something about her manner that was off. Ginger had never been physically affectionate or overly enthusiastic. She wasn't a girlie girl. My spidey-senses were on high alert, and I wondered if her strange manner was related to Nick.

"Ginger, hey. You look amazing. You remember my sister, August?" I introduced, because no matter how unsettled I felt, I was still British and I was brought up with good manners.

"Of course! August, so good to see you again. Tonight is going to be epic!"

Epic?! Okay, there was totally something going on.

"Are you okay? You seem a bit... different," I worded my concerns carefully, even as visions of Nick and Ginger in a passionate affair took over my mind.

"Me? Oh, I'm better than okay! I'm excited to be here!"

"Hmm. Okay. Have you seen Nick?" I asked. His seat at our table was empty. The only remaining seat on the table. How much more obvious could his absence be? My heart began to pound in my chest.

"Nick? Nick... oh, Nick? As in Santa? That Nick?" Ginger asked with a nervous laugh.

"Yes, that's the one. You know, your oldest friend in the world. The man you're closer to than anyone else, I guess?"

Ginger attempted to laugh, then sucked in a breath and descended into a coughing fit. "Ha! Yes, I forgot about him for a moment. Nope, you know, we really aren't that close lately. I haven't seen him in a hot minute. Anyway, I'd better find my seat. Excuse me, ladies."

I deliberately avoided August's gaze as I sat down next to her. I didn't want her sympathy. I was a single woman, I just hadn't had my status updated formally. My cheeks flamed as the event's MC took to the stage and asked everyone to take their seats.

"You'll be great," August leaned in and squeezed my hands.

I nodded. There was no way I could look at her without bursting into tears. She had that little sister magic way of looking at me and seeing straight to my soul.

"I'll now hand over to the organiser of this event, Dr Holly Wood!" The MC said, and the guests politely applauded as I carefully made my way to the stage.

I approached the microphone and looked out over the tables. The event had been a sell out, of course. Candy Cane Hollow loved a festive party, and the Winter Ball was the highlight in many a person's calendar.

"Good evening," I said. The microphone screeched its objection and I took a step closer. I'd given enough medical presentations to know that moving closer was always the answer, even when the microphone's argument made it seem as if you needed to back away.

"I'm Holly Wood, and I was tasked with the honour of organising this year's Winter Ball," I said. People applauded.

"Firstly, I must thank Mrs Claus for placing her trust in me. This is the first event I was asked to organise without her help, although I must admit that I did have help. The staff here at Festival Hall have worked tirelessly to put my plans into place, and for the last two days, my sister August has been here with me to help. If tonight disappoints you, that is my fault and my fault only. If tonight impresses you, it will be the hard working team who can take the credit for that."

I paused and joined the audience in clapping for the people who had worked so hard to make the event come to pass. They deserved every bit of recognition.

"With all of that said, I thought I'd end my speech with something a little different. August, can you join me?"

I looked out and watched as my beautiful sister planted a kiss on Jeb's cheek and handed him across to Tom, who looked awfully dapper in formal black tie attire.

Once August stood beside me on stage, we gave each other nervous smiles and began to sing the rest of the speech we had prepared.

"Last Christmas, I crashed my car
That very same day, I came here to stay
This year, to save me from tears
I'll travel instead by sleigh..."

The crowd went wild as we finished, and as I took my sister's hand in my own and looked out at the amazing community of people, I realised that I would get over losing Nick. Sure, I didn't want our relationship to end, but if he did for some reason, I could respect that and know that I had so much else going for me.

I grabbed August and gave her a hug, and so I missed whatever caused the whole audience to gasp.

We pulled apart, and there behind me was Nick, in his full Santa outfit. He gave me a nervous smile, and to my delight, his dimple grinned at me too.

I felt my heart pound in my chest. Surely he wasn't about to dump me on stage in front of the whole town?

I smiled back at him, because I had no control over what my face did when he was right there in front of me. I could barely hear a sound over the thumping of my heart.

I did catch sight out of the corner of my eye of August sneaking off stage, and vowed to tell her off for that later.

And then, right there in front of everyone who mattered to him, Nick dropped to one knee and looked up at me.

"I don't know if this is what you want for Christmas, but I do know it's what my mum is asking for this year. Holly, you are the love of my life and the Mrs Claus to my Santa. Will you do me the honour of being my wife?"

"Will I... you... your... marry you? Yes! Yes! Oh my gosh, a million times yes!" I exclaimed and I dropped to the floor before Nick could stand. I grabbed him and held on as if my life depended on it.

"You haven't even seen the ring," Nick whispered in my ear as I smothered his face with kisses.

"Are you kidding? I thought you were splitting up with me!" I admitted.

"Oh, Holly. Never. I've been so scared you might say no. And I thought if you looked at me, you'd see my plans written all over my face," Nick explained.

"Does Ginger know?" I asked.

"I had to tell someone, and I didn't think mum could keep it secret," he admitted. Well, that explained Ginger's odd behaviour earlier. To think I'd imagined that she was having an affair with Nick!

The two of us were pushed to the floor by the force of something like a rugby tackle, and neither of us needed to look to know that the impact was Mrs Claus joining our embrace.

"Oh, my dears! This is the best news ever! Have you picked a date yet?"

Nick and I laughed. Mrs Claus was going to be the ultimate Bridezilla, and that was absolutely fine by me.

We all managed to get to our feet, and worked the room to allow every person the chance to congratulate us on our engagement. Our engagement!

"Congrats, buddy. You've made a wise choice. I can tell you from experience, the Wood women are out of this world," Tom said as he high fived Nick. My heart swelled at the sight of them getting along.

"Thanks, man. I appreciate that. Also, I heard about your job news."

"Ah, yeah. It's a disappointment but these things happen."

"I could sure use someone with your experience over at Santa HQ if you'd have any interest? Think about it," Nick said.

"He'll take it!" August said with a shriek.

"He will?" Nick asked.

"Another thing I can tell you about the Wood women, Nick. They're always right. If August says I'll take it, I'll take it. When do I start?" Tom asked with a good natured grin.

Nick laughed. "As soon as you can get yourselves moved out here! The job's ready and waiting for you."

August and I grinned and hugged each other tight.

"Can you believe we're going to live in town together?" August asked.

"Can you believe how much Chanel you're going to get through?" I teased.

We all whooped as Michael Bauble took to the stage and began his set. It was going to be a night to remember, all right.

THE END
Get the next Christmas Mysteries book:
The Candy Cane Killer

ABOUT THE AUTHOR

Mona Marple is author of the Waterfell Tweed, Mystic Springs and Mexican Mysteries cozy mystery series, a co-author of the Witch in Time series, and author of this Christmas Mysteries series.

She lives in Nottinghamshire, England with her daughter, husband and pampered Labradoodle.

When she isn't writing words, Mona is probably reading them. She also enjoys walking, being by the sea, and spending quality time with her loved ones.

facebook.com/MonaMarpleAuthor

instagram.com/monamarple

Milton Keynes UK
Ingram Content Group UK Ltd.
UKHW022004130524
442669UK00018B/198/J